T

Lucy put her hands on either side of Victor's head and pulled his mouth down to hers. They kissed, a short and simple kiss, but when he raised his mouth from hers, she did not see a question in his gaze. He knew. She had invited him, and he knew it. She had vowed never to hurt him again, and she knew that to send him away from her bed this night would be to hurt him. She slid from under his arms, inching over in the bed, making room for him.

As he crawled under the blankets beside her, the light caught a pulse in his neck, a cadence to match her own pounding heart.

He leaned over her, kissing her again. She liked his kiss, and felt a strange quickening at the idea of receiving more. . . .

Praise for Teresa DesJardien

"Teresa DesJardien writes elegantly. . . . Her masterful touch is evident on every page."

—Mary Case Comstock

"One of the most original voices in the Regency genre."

—*Romantic Times*

The Marriage Masquerade

Teresa DesJardien

SIGNET
Published by New American Library, a division of
Penguin Putnam Inc., 375 Hudson Street,
New York, New York 10014, U.S.A.
Penguin Books Ltd, 80 Strand,
London WC2R 0RL, England
Penguin Books Australia Ltd, Ringwood,
Victoria, Australia
Penguin Books Canada Ltd, 10 Alcorn Avenue,
Toronto, Ontario, Canada M4V 3B2
Penguin Books (N.Z.) Ltd, 182–190 Wairau Road,
Auckland 10, New Zealand

Penguin Books Ltd, Registered Offices:
Harmondsworth, Middlesex, England

First published by Signet, an imprint of New American Library,
a division of Penguin Putnam Inc.

First Printing, December 2001
10 9 8 7 6 5 4 3 2 1

Printed in the United States of America

Author's Note

Buckingham House was formally titled "The Queen's House" by King George III, but many continued to refer to it by its former name, Buckingham House (named for its previous owner) throughout the Regency. Queen Charlotte lived there until her death in 1818.

Renovations to make it over into a royal residence for George IV were begun in 1825, the funds ran out in 1828, and George IV died in 1830, never having the chance to live in the royal home he was revamping for himself.

His brother, William IV, was the one to designate the building as Buckingham Palace, but he did not live long enough to reside there either. (Queen Victoria was the first monarch to make it her primary London residence.)

At the time of the Regency, the house was falling into ruin, and was a far smaller residence than it is currently. It was described as being no nicer than many a country manor in both its design and its size. Some of the rooms were known then by other names than how they are called today: The South Drawing Room is now known as the Blue Drawing Room; the Bow Room is now the Music Room.

Chapter 1

Lady Lucianne Gordon admired and loved her godmother, and normally would not wish to change much about the dear if often dour lady, but tonight she could wish her godmother was anyone but the queen of England. After all, the queen of England could do exactly as she wished—and tonight she wished to play matchmaker to her goddaughter.

"Ma'am," Lucianne murmured as she rose from her greeting curtsy to her godmother, "might I speak privately with you for a moment?"

"You may not," Queen Charlotte said with a coolness that did not necessarily denote unkindness.

The queen was, of course, entirely recognizable despite the jewel-encrusted black satin mask she wore and through which she eyed her goddaughter with regal assessment. Her German accent was still noticeable despite both the length of time she'd lived in England and her command of the language. Now in her seventieth year, her once-slim figure had thickened as a result of multiple births—fifteen children had lived to adulthood—and with age. She had never been a beauty, although once considered "fine," and age had not embellished what had not existed in youth. Her mouth, once described as a "mere slash," had perhaps softened a bit with time, even though she was not of the sort to freely hand out smiles.

She did not now smile at her goddaughter, but merely gave Lucianne the regal stare that silently said the queen's attention was ready to move on. There were many others, nearly all dressed in elaborate finery for the masquerade, waiting to make their bows to the queen.

Lucy had faced Godmama's stare many times before, however, and was not unduly intimidated by it, not when she now truly needed to speak with the queen. At least Godmother's gaze was relatively benign, unlike the stares that most people were turning Lucianne's way tonight. She felt their eyes on her, dragging at her shoulders as if their attention placed actual weight upon her. She knew that everyone who gaped at her was recalling the very strident, very vocal, and hideously public parting of the ways between Lucianne and her former fiancé, Mr. Jerome Holden, a little more than two weeks earlier.

The two of them had, not to mince words, conducted a shouting match in the middle of Hyde Park—an ugly, vulgar moment in the very heart of the fashionable world and during the most fashionable hour. There had been a hundred witnesses to the loud and odious row. Her shrieks had been from utter frustration—but they had also been a total disgrace.

Lucianne had fled to her family's town house, knowing she'd be compared to a Billingsgate fishwife or worse for the display of raw emotion she'd not been able to swallow. Never mind that Jerome had infuriated her . . . she ought not have responded to his insupportable boorishness with an even greater boorishness of her own. She was an earl's daughter, for goodness' sake, and while some might call her high-spirited, she'd never thought herself capable of screeching like a harridan—but screech she had.

Just remembering that ugly scene now made her want to turn and flee the masquerade. She'd not set a foot out of doors in the sixteen days since she'd quarreled so publicly with Jerome, and the only visitor she had been home to had been the queen's secretary, who had called twice—once right after Lucy's oh-so-public spat so that she might explain her behavior to the queen, and yet again just this morning. It had taken a written command from the queen to bring Lucy to this evening's occasion. She only wished the queen could also command away the humiliation and the whispers that Lucy had brought down on herself.

Lucy's mother, before her marriage, had been a lady-in-waiting to Queen Charlotte, a remarked favorite because she had a good command of the German language. The queen had, according to family legend, pouted a bit when she'd lost her favorite lady-in-waiting to marriage, but then later had graciously consented all the same to fill the role of godmother when the infant Lucianne had made her appearance.

Infant Lucianne and the queen, who liked babies far more than she did her own grown children, had quickly become enamored with each other. Their affection had survived Lucianne's youth and young adulthood, perhaps in part because Lucy had never grown out of petiteness. Her brother called her "Elf," in part because of her small stature and slender build, and partly for the shape of her face and her wide eyes and the chin that was more pointed than it was rounded.

Whatever its cause, the queen's partiality toward Lucianne had long pleased them both, and actually blossomed further when Lucy had made her come-out curtsy to the queen three seasons earlier.

Affection, however, was seldom what swayed Queen Charlotte when it came to decisions; she'd been at court too long to let such a paltry emotion guide her, Lucy knew. All the same, Lucy parted her lips to speak again, hoping reason might win out where royal affection was unlikely to.

Queen Charlotte did not give her the chance, interrupting crisply. "Lucianne, I've known you since you first drew breath. Were I to give you a chance to speak with me privately, I could very well tell you what you mean to say."

Lucy blushed to the roots of her nearly black hair, wishing this discussion were not taking place in so public a setting. People from the finest families, the bluest blood, and statesmen, honored guests from foreign climes, and military heroes were all present. It was a large and grand party, a masquerade, the rarest sort of party the queen ever hosted. Behind their masks, the queen's exalted guests looked out at Lucianne, and their finery only served to unnerve her further, to make their stares seem less kind and more judgmental.

Neither could Lucy miss the sibilance of whispers behind the fans of the queen's ladies, nor the disapproving gazes of her courtiers where they gathered, as always, around the queen. No doubt many of them considered Lucianne to be trying a doting godmother's regal patience.

But perhaps the queen sensed her goddaughter's growing unease, for despite having just denied Lucy a private word, she now motioned her goddaughter nearer. Their heads nearly touched as Lucy bent in toward the smallish throne that still managed to dominate one wall of the room.

The queen lowered her voice for Lucy's ears alone. "It won't serve, my girl. I'll not listen to any hen-hearted protests at this late date! We have an arrangement in place, and I mean to see it through."

"Please, Godmother, if you could pull any other name other than mine from the—"

The queen held up her hand, fingers stiff, instantly silencing Lucy with the gesture. "You agreed to this almost two weeks ago, Lucianne!" she said with quiet finality.

"I was distressed and—"

"Pish! My masquerade serves no purpose tonight other than to see that *you* are the one toasted and fêted, and not some other girl. Do I need to remind you that *you* are no longer betrothed? That you publicly embarrassed yourself? That you have begun your fourth season? *Fourth,* Lucianne! You are perilously close to being on the shelf." The queen gave a small, firm shake of her head. "The ruse goes forward—and you will cooperate."

Color suffused Lucy's face once more, for Godmother Charlotte had stated a decree—there was no changing her mind now. Lucy glanced at the various costumed persons surrounding the queen: ladies in waiting, gentlemen playing the part of courtier, the queen's friends, ministers, the inevitable toad-eaters—all the various personages a monarch's wife is constantly besieged by—and knew there was no way to further argue her point in front of all these people.

"Try to enjoy yourself, my dear girl," Queen Charlotte said quietly, patting Lucy's hands where they folded together pleadingly before the skirts of her masquerade costume.

Lucy knew the words for the dismissal they were, and took a step back to offer the curtsy she was expected to give at this point. She sent her godmother one last pleading look, but Queen Charlotte no longer deigned to look toward her goddaughter.

Lucy backed scarlet-faced into the crowd of other masquerade attendees, even as she slightly shook her head, stunned. How could she ever have agreed to participate in a fraud? What had possessed her to let the queen sweep aside her protests and good sense? How did she ever come to agree to play fast and loose with the truth . . . ?

Because there was nothing else to be done, Lucy pressed her hands into the multicolored folds of the troubadour-like gown she had donned in order to attend the queen's masquerade. Her left hand found the piccolo she carried in a fabric sheath that hung from her waist, but her mouth had gone too dry to play the instrument even if she'd felt so inclined. What to do now?

She glanced up, at first seeing no one she wished to speak to even though many of them were among the grandest names in the land, and almost all of them clad in lavish costume. Only one of the queen's five surviving daughters, Princess Sophia, was in attendance. She was dressed as a mermaid, fully clothed including long sleeves, the overskirt of her gown cleverly pulled to one side in a tail-like drape. Lucy's gaze swept on, over Lord Alvanley, currently one of the Prince of Wales's cronies and dressed as a monk, and the Almack's patronesses Lady Cowper and Princess Esterhazy, who were both in some manner of Grecian dress. She saw the poet Lord Byron, not in costume but all in black including his cravat and stockings, speaking with the Lord Mayor of the City, who—out of his usual fashion—bore a smile tonight along with his Crusader costume.

There were famous faces missing as well, not least of which was the monarch. Poor mad and now blind King George, currently caught between bouts of raving and utter silence in his sad, isolated world at Kew Palace.

His son, the Prince of Wales, was also notably absent, but that was hardly any surprise, for the prince and Queen Charlotte had long been estranged. She thought him frivolous, and he thought her overbearing, and the king's madness had done nothing to mend any rifts between them. His wife, the Princess Caroline, had almost certainly not even been sent an invitation, for the queen could not like the woman much more than did her son, who detested his wife. Many of the prince's frequent companions were missing as well: Richard Sheridan and Sir Francis Burdett were the two Lucy noted, whose politics the queen most certainly did not like. Beau Brummell would have been invited, but he had yet to make an appearance.

It was to none of these celebrated faces that Lucy looked, however, at last spying with relief her only brother, Reuben. She moved directly toward him, even while she thought that Reuben was quite unaware what lay ahead this night.

He had no idea that the queen had a little game in mind, a game of drawing names. One bowl would be filled with the names of eligible gentlemen, one with that of unmarried ladies. The queen would draw some man's name and match it with another name drawn from the bowl of female names . . . except that no matter what name the queen drew, she meant to read out *Lucy's* name. Lucy and the named fellow would then be dubbed Lord and Lady of the Masquerade and expected to spend the entire evening being at the center of the festivities.

Two weeks earlier, having been commanded to detail her public row with Mr. Holden to the queen, Lucy had promptly been informed that the queen thought her in desperate need of a social reforming.

"Your own younger sister is in danger of marrying before you," the queen had said, pointing out what Lucianne was already too aware of, "which is utterly insupportable. We *must* do something to present you in a fresh light to society, to accent your renewed eligibility! I have a little game in mind that should do the trick. It will certainly make you the center of attention at a little party I mean to throw . . ."

The "little party" had turned into a grand masquerade, with the cream of the *ton* invited—and Lucianne had allowed herself to be talked into attending it. Not just attending, but playing at being "surprised" when her name was called. Looking back now, Lucy was not entirely certain she had ever actually *agreed* to the scheme . . . but one was not required to agree with Godmother, only to obey.

Truth was, even Lucy quailed at the idea of facing society for a fourth season, and now in want of a beau. It made her look unwanted, unappreciated, like second takings.

In her first season she'd been deemed an Incomparable. Her form, while rounded enough for a young woman who would never be more than a half-inch above five feet, might have been a bit more endowed—but she had curves enough for her size. Her lack of height had worked to make her seem unique in a season rife with willowy young women. Her dark hair and ivory skin had been termed "enchanting." Her gray-green eyes had been labeled "captivating"—but she liked to think it was something of personal charm, and perhaps a ready smile, that had made her first season a success.

In her second season she had accepted a proposal of marriage from Jerome Holden, second son of a viscount. He was the most charming of men—it was easy to be enchanted by him, even if Lucy did not yet think of him as her beloved. Love would come, surely, once they were married? A woman of her station did not marry for love—but Lucy assumed she would come to care for Mr. Jerome Holden just as her parents clearly cared for each other.

From there she had cheerfully gone on into her third season, secure in the knowledge that she would marry when she and Jerome chose to set a date, and meanwhile they were free to enjoy what society had to offer.

There had been no hurry, no concerns. The rounds of parties, the dancing, the small flirtations, the delight of looking across the room and finding the one face you most hoped to see tonight . . . It had all been so pleasant, so entertaining—not to mention so fleeting a time of life. Why rush into marriage, with its obligations, its inevitable confinements, its curtailment of uncomplicated merriment? Life was sweet, they were young, and there was no unhappy gossip that needed to be quelled with the expediency of marriage.

The gossip had not existed until a little over two weeks earlier, when it became obvious that Lucy and Jerome Holden were not to marry after all—and then, all of a sudden, Lucy had found herself once again an "unattached" female, treacherously near to being perceived as an old maid.

She suspected she would not overly enjoy spinsterhood, if it came to that. And she was too well-born to go into service. She would be lucky to be hired, even if she wanted to be, for everyone else would also perceive her as too well-born; she'd be out of her assigned place in life, a very suspicious thing indeed. No, Lucy must marry. It was the best future for her, since the only other option was spinsterhood and living forever with her parents. She was an earl's daughter. Marriage had been decreed since the moment of her birth, and it behooved her to do her duty.

Too, the queen was right—for the sake of form it would be best if Lucy married before her younger sister. Rebecca, after all, was already all but betrothed to Mr. Ellis, and this was just her first season!

Now, the sight of Reuben's calm, unaware features caused Lucy to lower her shoulders and issue a resigned sigh. There was no getting out of it. She must allow herself to be put forward by the queen, must be deemed "Lady of the Masquerade." The queen hoped to thrust her goddaughter back into the center of attention, "where one may best be seen and best make an attachment," as she'd assured Lucy.

Which meant, Lucy supposed, that she would have to make the most of the evening, even if she hated how the event was to be deliberately arranged. The truth, not wrapped up in clean linen, was that she required a new fiancé, and the only way to obtain one was to be "seen."

A fiancé, a marriage—then love to follow, that's how it should go. Lucy frowned a little at the niggling feeling that she was being too logical, too levelheaded, that something was missing in this equation, but now was not the time to second-guess. There was nothing to do but get through what promised to be a long evening.

She fixed a smile on her face and lifted her chin, determined to meet the challenge with at least a show of aplomb.

She had almost reached Reuben's side when he slipped away through a door. She could only presume he was going outside to smoke one of his cigarillos.

Lucy sighed, realizing she was at least temporarily

on her own. She fixed a new smile in place, then moved to join the throngs that had come to attend the queen's masquerade, hoping no one noticed she moved with all the stiffness of someone approaching the gallows.

Victor, Lord Oxenby, looked down the street to glance at his destination: Buckingham House, or as it was more formally called, the Queen's House. It had once been a fine home, if perhaps a shade less grand than most large country houses, but now signs of decline were everywhere. The gardens were still tended, but their tidy confines only served to punctuate the general air of decrepitude of the house itself. Here was a cracked window, there a visibly rotting sill, and there a rusty stain that traced from the roofline to the ground. The king had never seen fit to fund repairs, reflecting either his usual parsimony or his encroaching fits of madness.

It was not the house that caught Victor's attention, however, but a familiar figure leaning against a bit of fence that marked the end of the Queen's House property, smoking a cigarillo. It was Reuben, more formally known by his courtesy title of Viscount Heshmont, an earl's son and Victor's closest friend. He was in costume, although Victor was hard pressed to say what manner of costume it was.

Victor caught his friend's eye and both men lifted a hand in greeting.

Although pleased enough to approach his friend, Victor altered the pattern and pace of his steps—not for Reuben's sake, but because of the guards posted before the royal residence. There were very few persons who had seen Victor's true walk, or even seen him make use of the cane he carried for fashion. The bones of his lower right leg had healed wrong after the accident. They hurt less if he walked with his usual gait, but with a bit of concentration he could turn his limp into a kind of dandyish swagger, and his cane was almost always tucked under his arm instead of put to actual use. If people therefore put down his leisurely pace to a kind of sophisticated ennui, they were welcome to do so. It was a poor enough thing that the long-ago accident was clearly marked by the large Y-shaped scar across the right side of his face; he didn't need to emphasize the limp that went with it.

A horse's hoof had left him thus marked, the same horse that had mangled his leg. He'd been eight years old, a little apprehensive of the huge creature whose reins he'd been told by Father to hold. Something had happened—it was guessed that one of the dogs had dashed after some vermin, so intent on its prey that it possibly ran under or at least brushed against the horse. Regardless, the horse had spooked and reared, and its heavily shod feet had come down on top of Victor. If his father had not caught the reins almost at once and turned the bucking creature aside, it was assumed that Victor would have been killed.

Instead, he had a leg that ached when he asked too much of it, and an extensive scar on his face. It ran from almost the right corner of his mouth to just below his right eye, with a second scar tracing from the first toward his ear. He looked in his mirror and knew that he would have been considered handsome were it not for that scar. His bone structure and teeth had all been retained, and he knew he should feel grateful for those boons, but he was not blind to how the scar managed to make his face look uneven, lacking balance. It was red and rather jagged, and his skin had proven to be the sort that did not heal well and easily, but poorly and markedly. The scar was neither dashing as some men's scars managed to be, nor nobly won in war. It was just ugly.

He hated explaining that he'd merely been trampled by a horse. Fortunately the question had ceased to be asked often anymore, since he'd made London his primary residence after father's death and his gaining his majority, and everyone had long since heard the tale.

To this day he thought of horses as little more than a ubiquitous and somewhat evil necessity. He tolerated being driven in a carriage, when he must, but he never rode astride. He did not trust the beasts, with their tossing heads, their easily spooked natures, and their equine brains that sometimes had plans of their own. He'd rather walk, rather have to put his leg up at night with hot compresses. London suited him very well, for there he could walk to most any event or shop he wished, or be ferried there by boat. Even during the few summer weeks he spent at his country estate, he preferred strolling over driving. When he must make use of a carriage, it was his coachman who drove, not Victor.

He knew this made him the oddest of men, for every one of his acquaintances was mad for the creatures, be it acquiring a new team for their latest carriage, or for the races, or purchasing a fashionable mount for riding in the park. Victor did not care. If he had to stand near one of the beasts, it created in him a soul-deep panic that made his hands shake, made sweat bead on his brow, and made his breathing become too rapid and shallow. He knew it was absurd, but he avoided the animals if at all possible all the same.

"You arrive fashionably late," his friend called out to him now. Reuben took a final inhalation from his cigarillo before tossing it down and grounding it out with the toe of his boot.

"I would not have arrived at all were anyone but the queen hosting this masquerade," Victor said in a sour tone as he stepped to his friend's side.

"What manner of creature are you?" Reuben asked, looking dubious as he indicated Victor's ensemble, which was a bright red waistcoat under a flurry of feathers sewn to a dark brown coat and breeches. Yellow stockings and brown dancing pumps completed his attire.

"I am Cock Robin," Victor said, feigning a frown. "You could not tell?"

"A nursery tale bird? Where's your hat?"

"Hat?" Victor scoffed.

"Well, something with feathers on it, or a bill of some sort, to make you look like a bird."

"Don't be ridiculous."

Reuben eyed his friend. "Oh, *I* am ridiculous? At least I am not wearing any feathers."

"True. But what are you?"

"A maharajah."

Victor lifted his brows, comment enough.

Reuben laughed. "Bedclothes twisted over my breeches and a few baubles around my neck do not suffice to give the illusion?" he asked.

"Your appearance is . . . unique," Victor said, now also grinning, feeling the familiar pull of his scar near his mouth.

"Not the descriptive word I would have hoped for," Reuben said dryly.

The two men turned with unspoken accord, striding toward the formal path that would lead them to the entrance of the queen's residence.

"So you do not care for masquerades?" Reuben commented. "I thought everyone liked to don a costume now and again."

"I suppose I always feel a bit disappointed, that's

all," Victor said lightly. "When was the last time you actually wondered who was behind the mask they wear? And only one lady in recent memory has bothered to disguise her voice, and yet I could tell at once it was Lettice Falconer."

Reuben nodded. "Her lisp."

Victor gave one brief nod as well. He would have gone on, but a roughly clothed man stepped down from a tattered old curricle and intercepted them.

"I'll be having yer purses and watches now, gentlemun," the man growled at them, holding out both hands, one to receive what he'd demanded and the other holding a knife.

Reuben stared, perhaps not quite comprehending for a moment, but Victor did not pause. He brought up his walking stick, slashing it across the man's face, and brought it down again almost at once, with force, across the wrist of the hand holding the knife. The knife fell to the ground, as did the man, who screamed out in pain.

"Me face!" he cried as Victor kicked the knife well out of the man's reach and stepped on the back of his head, pinning the man to the ground.

"He meant to rob us!" Reuben cried, looking back and forth between his friend, the prone man, and the curricle waiting so the man might make his escape. "God save us, Victor, I knew you were good with your fists, but I never thought to see such work with a walking stick!" he said with admiration. "I pray I never have to have a go-round with you. You're a wonder, you are."

Victor had heard such praise before, for a boy with a scarred face did not grow into manhood without encountering bouts of fisticuffs brought on by insults. However, Victor's domination in such scuffles had quickly grown, to the point where eventually he'd had no need to actually fight anymore, his reputation at being well able to defend himself preceding him.

Reputation for strength and dexterity in a fight nonetheless, Victor was just about to suggest that Reuben could be of better assistance were he to help hold the scoundrel down, when a quick glance showed him that a half dozen royal guards were already at hand. They'd no doubt noted the altercation, being quick to react to a to-do so close to the queen's residence.

Not fifteen minutes later, Victor and Reuben were admitted through the single door that was the front entrance of the Queen's House. They moved up the wide stairs to the open door of the Bow Room, where a multicolored and festooned group of masqueraders crowded. The footpad who had tried to rob them was already on his way to Newgate, his curricle confiscated, and Reuben still shaking his head in disbelief at the attack.

"Wait until I tell Lucy about this—" he began, but Victor interrupted him at once.

"Pray, do not."

"Why ever not?"

Victor lifted his chin, indicating a direction, and Reuben followed his gaze. Lucy stood not twenty feet away, frowning slightly and looking pale. "She appears already distressed by something," Victor pointed out.

Victor's second glance at his friend's sister proved him correct. Her hands were knotted together before her, and she stood alone, not in a group of friends as she would normally be. Victor watched a stab of regret cross Reuben's face, no doubt for having left her side long enough to indulge in blowing a cloud—it couldn't be easy for her, now that most of London had heard tale of her broken engagement. Even though it was reportedly she who had broken the betrothal, somehow there still hung an air of rejection about her. Lady Lucianne had always been a bright spot at any party, always well received—she was not used to playing the part of "unchosen." The experience clearly baffled her and left her at something of a loss—and even her brother, who was fond of his little sister, winced to see her in such obvious agitation.

"You should go to her side," Victor counseled.

"Both of us," Reuben said. "Make it look as though she's surrounded by friends. We'll get some other people to—"

"I am not her friend," Victor said, feeling regret, as always, despite the truth of the words.

Chapter 2

Victor watched his friend walk toward Lady Lucianne, struck as always by how much taller Reuben was than his sister. Then again, almost everyone was taller than Lady Lucianne. However, her lack of height took nothing away from how fetching she looked in her costume with its jaunty little troubadour's hat.

Victor sighed. It would have served no purpose for him to join Reuben at the lady's side, for Lady Lucianne would have failed to be comforted by his presence. She and he had been acquaintances since he had met Reuben a dozen years earlier, but some four years or so ago the acquaintanceship between himself and Lucy had faltered, never evolving into friendship.

It was not that Victor did not like Lady Lucianne. *Indeed,* he thought with a grim smile, *I like her very well.* He'd liked her since she had been a mere ten-year-old and he the rather thick-skulled age of fourteen; even at such tender ages, Victor had known there was something uniquely "right" about Lady Lucianne Gordon. Even then she'd had a smile that captured one's breath . . . and Victor was not entirely sure he'd released it since.

Even though their association had grow irrevocably cooler with the years—it'd be fairer to call it icy cold—Victor was not blind to Lady Lucianne's many graces. She was a petite thing, saved, at second glance, from appearing childlike by gentle womanly curves that suited her small frame. She had a manner that, while often gay and lighthearted, was hardly juvenile. She had a piquant little face—Reuben sometimes called her "Elf"—but somehow her delicate features and pointed chin managed to be a woman's face. Victor supposed it was the evident intelligence in her gaze that did the trick. She also possessed warmth, wit, an elegance of carriage that many a stage dancer might have envied, and a calmness of nature that was much more attractive than the practiced elan some young women affected. Then, of course, there was the charm of her smile.

Not that she has ever directed that smile my way, Victor thought. *And not that our estrangement is any real fault of hers,* he concluded with a rueful shake of his head. He'd handled an awkward moment so poorly that it had turned from mere poor timing into a disaster, an ugly moment that had created total disaffection with each other. He even knew why he had done it: that besides liking Lucianne Gordon's personality and manner, he'd been powerfully attracted to her in a sexual sense ever since she'd stepped out of the schoolroom and into society four years ago.

He'd been attracted to any number of women before, of course, but it had always been either a matter of his heart or sudden passion being touched—not both at once. But when Lady Lucianne had come down her father's stairs one evening, in the pretty and grown-up-looking white dress of a miss making her come out, her hair still plaited but now pinned atop her head, Victor had known a sudden and unlooked-for shock of deep attraction. Not just an attraction for her physical person, but a strangely deep longing that was almost painful.

He'd known her for years, had tugged her plaits just to hear her squeal, knew her laugh, knew what she looked like in a pout. But this night she was both familiar and different, and he'd found himself longing to hear her laugh anew, at something he said, something that made her turn her wide eyes up to meet his own.

A little time spent at her side that evening had quickly shown him that the girl he'd always liked had turned into a pretty, witty woman with whom he could all too easily fall in love.

Their childhood association had dissipated that night, and in its place had formed a chasm that seemed to widen, day after day—a chasm largely of Victor's own making, one that grew from him not wanting Lady Lucianne to know of the strong allure she held for him. Their acquaintance had until then been cordial if indifferent, for she had been little more to him than the younger sister of his friend—but now he'd seen her as a woman grown.

He'd known at once that his attraction was never the thing, could never be allowed to grow; he was of lesser birth than she. His funds might be healthy, but with her dowry she could marry so much better than a mere baron, and a *nouveau* one at that. Not to mention that she was pretty, young, and rich enough not to need to marry just anyone, such as a man with a stiff leg and a large jagged scar on his face.

He had never acted on the deep attraction he felt toward her (not outside the occasional brief flight of fancy anyway) nor did he harbor any illusions that he ever could. He was not meant to be at Lady Lucianne's side. That was just reality, so he'd best accept the idea.

One night, he'd allowed himself to imbibe deeply of the excellent port to be had at his club. Well into his cups, he'd announced to the world that he meant to be a bachelor forever, that he had no use for a bride in his life. He'd awakened the next day to several regrets, but his pronouncement had not been one of them. He knew he could find some woman who would accept him to husband, scar, limp, and all—but it had been something of a relief to have chosen the unmarried state, to have made a decision. He'd never uttered one thing contrary to the matter since.

Married, unmarried. Attraction, rejection. What did it all matter anyway? Never mind he and Lady Lucianne had had their final falling-out shortly before she'd become betrothed, that she'd turned her charming smile elsewhere. It only mattered at the moment because it meant his presence at her side tonight would offer her no solace.

Nor did it matter that the lady's very presence in the room still held the ability to make his heart squeeze painfully. It was enough that she was safely ensconced at Reuben's side, and Victor was free to turn to the reason he'd come tonight: to please Queen Charlotte. He moved into the queue that waited to be presented to her, making an effort not to glance over at Lady Lucianne in her multicolored troubadour's ensemble.

"Your Majesty," he greeted his monarch's consort when his turn came. He rose from his bow before the low-backed throne in which she sat. She was dressed as a noblewoman of some centuries past, Italian perhaps, an elaborate peaked hat upon her head. She wore a jeweled mask that covered her eyes, but there was of course no mistaking who she was. Indeed, only about half the guests had bothered to wear masks, and only a handful of them had tried to disguise themselves—one *wished* to be seen at the queen's masquerade, an invitation that could only enhance one's significance. Even before he had fallen ill, King George and his queen seldom entertained at their home, preferring to conduct social or state events at St. James's Palace. An invitation to this event at the Queen's House was rarer than gold.

Queen Charlotte inclined her head, the hat staying firmly in place as though to reflect her regal dignity. With a bow, Victor accepted this as both acknowledgment and dismissal, but before he could move aside, she chose to greet him verbally, an honor not bestowed on everyone. "Oxenby," she said crisply, eyeing his Cock Robin costume with a royal skepticism she could not keep from her features. "You are late in arriving at my masquerade!"

"Your Majesty," he answered with a slight smile, prepared to share an old joke, "it is how an upstart such as myself achieves notice."

One of the queen's ladies-in-waiting gasped at his reply, even though she must surely have long heard that Queen Charlotte had dubbed the third Lord Oxenby "an upstart" at their very first meeting. For her part, the queen did not respond with an answering smile, but Victor saw one gleaming in her eyes.

At the age of one-and-twenty he had come into his majority, then able to take his seat in the House of Lords. He had also, for the first time, been invited to attend the king's levee. The king, however, had fallen too ill (some said he'd gone into a breathless rant, in one of his "fits" again) to greet his subjects. Queen Charlotte, visibly agitated, had arrived at the levee to pronounce her husband's absence, greeting each of the young men in attendance in place of her ailing husband.

"Your Majesty," Victor had said after bowing to his queen, murmuring his greetings, and receiving a weary nod. "Might I fetch a dish of tea for you?" He'd had the good sense not to tell her she looked tired and undoubtedly perturbed by her husband's newest bout with mania, but the suggestion was implicit in the offer.

She had said a great deal with just one haughty glance at him: that she had servants and ladies aplenty to fetch whatever she might need; that he had been presumptuous to think she might require the reinforcement of tea; that despite those truths he had managed to please her. He suspected it did not occur to many of her subjects to offer her whatever they would offer anyone else in similar distress. At any rate, it was clear that his spontaneous offer had not offended.

"You may not," she had intoned dryly, almost causing him to doubt the impression he'd gotten, but then she had smiled just a little. "Upstart!" she had dubbed him with a tiny wrinkling of her nose, a gesture that made him think that perhaps King George was not so mad after all since he always had been devoted to the woman.

"Upstart" his queen had said—and he'd been unable to deny the truth of the designation. His grandfather had supplied good quality shot to the Royal Army, and consequently late in life had made a fortune. A grateful king had also granted him a title to go with that fortune, both of which prizes the first Lord Oxenby had passed on at his demise, only a year later, to his own son. Fifteen years after that, Victor's father had succumbed to a wasting disease, making Victor the baron, the Oxenby title being of a mere sixteen years' duration.

No one was more aware of his *nouveau* status than Victor himself. Indeed, he'd promised his papa on the man's deathbed that he'd do all he could to raise up and promote the Oxenby name, to erase the smell of commerce that still clung to the name. It was that very promise that had brought him to sit in the House, to play the part of nobleman, to take bachelor's rooms in the City. He *was* an upstart, just as the queen claimed—so how to answer the pronouncement?

The gleam she could not hide in her eyes was all the answer he needed, though. "Your Majesty," he said, "I am pleased to have you call me thus, for the very great advantage of being an upstart is that one is utterly inclined to be of service."

Her eyes had narrowed, but not in disapproval, for she laughed aloud, a short bark. "An upstart with a glib tongue! But I think you are no flatterer, Oxenby." She had eyed him up and down, including a frank appraisal of his scarred face, and with a breathless clarity he'd realized his fate at court, his very reputation in London, hung on her next words.

"Since you are clearly too plainspoken to play at courtier," she said, her regal tranquility now back in place as she opened a fan and began to leisurely waft it before herself, "I shall not ask you to attend me here at court. But I do have a duty for you, sirrah."

Victor tilted his head, a questioning gesture that urged her to continue.

"I ask," she had said, "that you always be plainspoken with me. I ask that you be my friend."

"Your Majesty," Victor had said, his voice thick with an unexpected depth of emotion, "it would be my very great pleasure," he'd stated with complete honesty.

He had gone on, indeed, to become the lady's friend—or as much of one as a subject can be to his queen. By living outside the daily commotion of royal existence, he remained largely untouched by it; he believed he served, in a small way, as both friend and fresh air to her. He never regurgitated court rumors, or indeed any rumors, nor asked after her sons' various misdeeds or excessive expenses, but only spoke with her as he did his own mother, telling his queen the news of his own day. He spoke of a new hat he had bought, or a new bootblack his valet had discovered, or a hundred other droll things. He was fairly certain she enjoyed the change, the deliberate lack of state or worldly issues, and that he put no real demands upon her time or favor.

In honor of their first encounter, he'd never adopted the style of calling her "Ma'am" as was usual after salutations had been satisfied, but instead always used the more formal "Your Majesty." She had allowed it, not to keep him in his place, but out of an unspoken shared point of humor. She would forever be "Your Majesty" to him just as he would forever be her "upstart."

For her part, the queen's rare and patent approval of him had done what he could not have done half so well by himself, no matter how charming he had made an effort to be: He had been welcomed into society. Oh, perhaps not the highest heights—he had yet to receive a voucher for Almack's, for instance, despite his "royal connection"—but all the same the Oxenby name had a new, clearly more agreeable scent about it, even if its owner bore an unsightly scar upon his face.

So when Queen Charlotte invited him to attend a masquerade she cared to throw, there had never been a moment of doubt as to Victor's attendance.

"We are to play a game tonight," the queen told him now, even while she glanced to see who waited in line behind him to make their bows. "I want my game to look wildly successful," she said frankly, loud enough to be overheard. "Be sure you participate, Oxenby. *All* the unmarried men must participate," she said with a hint of steel.

"I will, Your Majesty," he said quite unnecessarily, for they both knew he had already been dismissed and had no opportunity to demur now even if he had reason to. Neither would any other eligible gentleman refuse to play, he felt sure. He had scarcely stepped aside before the queen was already nodding to Lord Hamley, who had been waiting behind him, costumed as a shepherd.

Victor stepped back into the perpetual circle around the queen, lingering there among a profusion of bright costumes, jewels, and fanciful wigs, long enough to hear the unmarried Lord Hamley equally commanded to play the queen's game.

Victor turned away, looking about in hopes of finding a glass of wine before this game—was there anything as tedious as a party game?—must be endured. For the queen's sake, no matter the tedium, he would play the part of good sport.

To his surprise, when the queen's majordomo moved to the center of the Bow Room and rapped his staff on the floor to command the attention of everyone in the hall, the game that was proposed was hardly onerous. At least, it would only prove to be onerous for one unlucky couple.

"Her Royal Majesty will be choosing two persons, one male and one female, to serve us tonight as Lord and Lady of the Masquerade," the majordomo intoned loudly in order to be heard over the general hubbub. He pointed at two servants, one on either side of him. "To my right is the bowl for ladies' names. To my left is the bowl for gentlemen's names. Circulating among you are other servants with paper and ink, so that all unmarried adult persons may inscribe their name upon a piece of paper, which is to be folded twice and placed into the appropriate bowl. Please write only your own name. Also please refrain from entering the drawing more than once."

Murmurs swept through the crowd as paper and quills were brought forth and put to use, and laughter scattered through the room as various persons were urged to put their name in the provided bowls. One fellow half bent at the waist, offering this back as a writing surface to several young ladies, and several others went about collecting the bits of paper, offering to place them in the bowls.

When a servant handed Victor a paper and ink-dipped quill, he made use of a nearby table, wrote "Oxenby" with a flourish, and sent his slip of paper toward the bowl via an acquaintance who offered to carry it there with his own.

"Lord Oxenby," hailed a nearby fellow who looked particularly young in a Robin Hood costume. Victor thought a moment and came up with a name: Harold Farwynn, the son of one of his mother's good friends.

"Farwynn," he acknowledged.

"I certainly hope it is not my name that is called," young Farwynn said, indicating the bowls of names with a movement of his chin.

"I hope that it is," Victor said with a grin. "For then it shan't be mine."

The young man smiled in return. "I'd feel a perfect fool. It's not poor enough that my sisters insisted I had to dress thus, all in green down to my shoes, but to be paraded around as Lord of the Masquerade? No, thank you."

Victor nodded, in perfect sympathy with the sentiment. "Perhaps some other unlucky person will get to look the fool, and we'll enjoy the masquerade all the more at his expense, eh?"

The youth grinned again, but then their attention shifted to the queen, who had risen to her feet as the two servants with bowls approached her.

"I should warn the participants that they must do their part to make this a festive occasion!" she said, a gentle scold. "We mean to celebrate you and fête you and make you the center of all attention, all evening long. You must rule, leading us in a merry fashion, setting the dances, suggesting entertainments, and otherwise making sure we all have reason to lift our glasses in salute to the Lord and Lady of the Masquerade at evening's end. At midnight, those who have masks will remove them and earn a kiss for their trouble, and then we shall make merry until dawn!" the queen pronounced.

Her words must have been a prearranged clue, for as a wave of applause rippled through the crowd, one of the servants stepped forward. He went down on one knee, offering the bowl up to Her Majesty.

"First, the Lady of the Masquerade shall be announced!" bellowed the majordomo.

Queen Charlotte reached into the bowl, mixing the bits of paper with one hand, making the pronouncement wait upon a small dramatic pause. At length she drew a paper and unfolded it. "The Lady of the Masquerade is . . . Lady Lucianne Gordon!" she announced.

"Oh, no," Victor murmured. Lady Lucianne might be a callow little thing, but she was far from villainous. She had already been distressed about something tonight—Victor could not imagine that this command into a public performance would please her. Nor could he miss that mere polite applause met the announcement, not the thunderous sound Victor would have expected just a few weeks ago. Once the pinnacle of all that was in the mode, Lady Lucianne's name now brought only lukewarm approval.

The young man next to him made a face. "Poor girl. Not as well received as she had been, is she? Did you hear about that scene in Hyde Park? And, I mean to say, a fourth season? It makes you wonder a bit, don't it? She's an earl's daughter! Word is her dowry's sizable. I'd think she'd have a dozen new suitors lined up, except everyone wonders if she's a termagant, don't you think?" Farwynn thus summed up all the talk that Lucianne Gordon had to know was being whispered behind fans.

"Oh, I do not know," Victor said in a half-bored tone, for he knew to protest too much was only likely to confirm rather than deny such tattle. "It could be that there is something queer with the *fellow,* and Lady Lucianne had the good sense to see it and call off any wedding to him."

"Holden?" the youth queried, looking startled. "Nah, he's a right go'er, he is. I've met him. A proper Corinthian."

Victor felt his lips go thin, and he mentally shook his head. The problem was, most of London would wholly agree with the young man. The Honorable Jerome Holden, second son of a marquess (and who was likely to inherit the title one day from his older brother, who had delicate lungs) *was* everything Mr. Farwynn had named him to be, wholly embraced by society. If he was a bit too outlandish at times, a bit too unsteady in his demeanor, a bit too puffed up with his own importance—society expected no less from "a right go'er."

No less so, now that he had thrown over his family's protests and galloped off to fight in the war. His actions were seen as heroic—as indeed, Victor supposed, they were. The man's family had wanted him to stay far from battle, as the heir's health was fragile, but Holden had defied any such waiting role and instead bought a commission.

Of course, underlying his own impressions of Holden, Victor resented the man for the single phrase Reuben had uttered upon revealing the dissolution of Lucianne's betrothal: "He never gave her wishes a thought."

An apparent spell of thoughtlessness was hardly enough on which to condemn the man—but Victor could not like Mr. Jerome Holden regardless of his popularity or his answering of the call to duty. He was glad Lady Lucianne had thrown the inconsistent, swaggering braggart over. She deserved someone better, someone not so narrow in his thinking even while being so flamboyant in his nature.

"I wish I could say congratulations," said Mr. Farwynn at his side, a rueful half smile on his face.

"Beg your pardon?" Victor said, returning to the moment with a small shake of his head.

"I didn't think you'd heard," Mr. Farwynn said. "Your name was selected from the bowl for gentlemen."

Victor's gaze flew to the queen, who did not look at him as she returned to her seat—but everyone else in the hall had turned to face him. He knew in a flash that Mr. Farwynn had only spoken the truth. "Good gad!"

The queen looked at him then, lifting an imperious hand to demand he cross to her side. Another quick glance told Victor that Lady Lucianne already stood there, her face gone pale as milk. The dainty lady was not pleased, not at all. He could read her displeasure in the set of her shoulders—and who could blame her? Who was to be glued to her side all night but the one man who had disparaged her in front of others?

Moving as unnaturally as a marionette, his mind whirling, Victor strode toward the queen's chair. He felt foolish in his Cock Robin apparel, feathers fluttering as he moved. By the time he reached her side, his lips had already parted to speak.

The queen interrupted him before he could, however, seizing his hand and pulling him down to plant an airy, regally formal kiss on his cheek while an errant feather sewn to the shoulder of his coat brushed her mask. "Do not embarrass my goddaughter by refusing this one night of simple duty to me!" she hissed in his ear before she set his hand free, her German accent having deepened as it did when she was agitated.

He stepped back, glanced at the grim expression on Lady Lucianne's face, and realized his queen had a point. To protest, to ask that the queen draw another woman's name, was to insult Lady Lucianne. An evening in her least favorite person's company was a poor enough offering for the lady, but to have that person refuse to keep *her* company . . . ! Victor could not do it.

For Lady Lucianne's sake, for Reuben and the queen's sake—even for the sake of his own reputation as a gentleman of some manners and wit—Victor must smile, nod, and bear it.

Swallowing the protest he'd been about to offer, Victor said instead to Queen Charlotte: "Your Majesty, how do we begin?"

Her expression scarcely changed, except that perhaps her small smile became more sincere. "Why, you two must open the dancing, of course," she replied as she rose once more to her feet.

"You are cordially invited," called out the majordomo, "to join Her Majesty Queen Charlotte in the South Drawing Room, for dancing."

Victor bit back another comment, a protest that he did not often dance due to his injured leg. He *could* dance, if not entirely smoothly, if he were careful to avoid any set that involved sudden pivots. He'd not fallen yet on a public dance floor . . . and he hoped tonight would not be an exception to that good fortune.

The queen began to lead the way from the room, but she stopped abruptly, her daughter nearly colliding with her from behind. The queen turned just enough to be able to cast a speaking glance toward Lady Lucianne.

Victor took the hint. "My Lady of the Masquerade?" he said formally as he stepped to Lucy's side. He offered her a feather-covered arm.

Her eyes rounded slightly, revealing she was well aware the queen offered the two of them a precedence they did not normally deserve. They were to enter the ballroom just behind the queen and then Princess Sophia. Victor had certainly never seen it done before—not with two dukes, a handful of war heroes, and a bevy of important city fathers among the crowd. He swallowed, suddenly anxious that this "honor" of being made lord of the evening's entertainment might prove even more taxing than he'd feared.

As for Lucianne, her expression grew carefully blank now, and she accepted his arm without demur.

The threesome moved as a unit into the South Drawing Room, where a large contingent of musicians waited, crowded into a corner.

"Your Majesty, do you care to dance?" Victor asked, even though he would have been surprised if she had accepted. She had once adored dancing, but age had taken its toll. She did not dance often these days—besides, it was abundantly obvious she meant to take advantage of having drawn her goddaughter's name. Victor's stomach flip-flopped as he thought again that it was the most unfortunate pairing of names, his and Lady Lucianne's, not only because they were *not* friends, but also because the queen was too clever a female to let opportunity slip away. What might have been a simple party game, had every chance now of turning into a major "advance the Lady Lucianne" event—and he was caught in the middle of it.

"I will not dance," the queen informed him. "Please take me to that chair, there, and you will open the dancing with Lucianne."

He *could* say no. It was not too late. He could recall an urgent task he needed to attend to. Victor glanced between the two women. For the one he felt gratitude and real affection; for the other he felt, as ever, the half-delicious sting of attraction mingled with the prick of their estrangement. Normally he would keep himself far from her company, but it was too late for that. There was no need to be unduly unkind. He must make it his business to be cordial, if cool, and to do nothing to distress her further this night.

There was only one answer he could give, and he hoped he did so graciously. "Yes, Your Majesty."

He saw the queen settled in the chair she had indicated, her ladies and hangers-on sweeping around her once more, and then everyone else stood respectfully while the musicians played "God Save the King." This was followed by the inevitable small cheers of "huzzah!" and "indeed!" and then the musicians struck up the quadrille.

Victor turned to Lady Lucianne. He realized that he had never danced with her before, that her dainty stature made him feel quite tall even though he was an inch shorter than Reuben. He bowed before offering his hand to lead her into the dance, hoping any regrets were now firmly hidden.

She hesitated for just one long moment, but it was long enough that Victor doubted few had missed it or the reluctance of which it spoke. Still, a moment later she had placed her hand in his and they were striding to the center of the dance floor.

Victor positioned his feet, even while he glanced around the room. Just as he'd feared, it was obvious that he and Lady Lucianne were not only to begin the set, but to do so as the only couple. Others would join in eventually, but for now everyone stood back to observe the Lord Cock Robin and the Lady Troubadour perform the opening to the dancing.

"I am so sorry," Lady Lucianne said as they waited for the prelude to conclude. She spoke very quietly, her lips scarcely moving, so that only he could hear.

"Sorry?" he replied in like manner.

"That you had to be paired with me. That your name was called. It is the worst luck."

Even while one part of him listened for the beat of the music in order to take the cue and begin dancing, he felt his face bloom with heat that she could be so frank in her disgust of him.

"It is only one night." The words were ground out. "I assure you I will not bother you further once this sad little event is over, if that is what you fear."

Lady Lucianne gave a gasp, causing him to glance at her. He was surprised to find distress written across her features.

"You think I meant to insult you!" she whispered. "But that is not what I meant. I meant it was the worst luck for *you*."

He stared at her, and only because she took a step

forward did he realize he'd missed the first beat of the dance. He compensated, and then there was no time to pursue her odd comment as they moved through the motions of the dance, each of them avoiding the other's gaze to cast a false smile toward the crowd watching them so keenly.

Chapter 3

As their dance continued, Lucy kept her eyes open wide, hoping that eventually the excess moisture there would dry and never turn into a tear to slide down her cheek. She was certain she must have the most extraordinary expression on her face, but there was nothing for it; she could not be seen wiping away tears. Her godmother had gone to a great deal of trouble on her part, and she would not be so ungrateful as to ruin the queen's plans even if she wished they'd never been implemented.

It was just that of all the people Lucy could have been paired with . . . Lord Oxenby! The only man to ever openly show his contempt of her.

All the same, the deed could not be undone. His name had been chosen and called out, and the evening must be got through. Besides, tears would only grant Lord Oxenby all the more reason to dislike her. It was bad enough that he had misunderstood her apology—one she ought not to have muttered aloud, she knew that now. It was impossible for her to explain that her regrets sprang from sharing in the queen's duplicity, and not from Oxenby's name being matched with hers. She had clearly added insult to injury, but with no way to explain herself.

Neither did it signify that the queen would be

vastly disappointed if she thought an evening together would produce any attraction between Lucy and her evening's captive and reluctant companion. It was unlikely to produce even a civil conversation, let alone an affinity.

Never mind, she thought. The real purpose behind the evening was not to attract the "Lord of the Masquerade's" attention; it was to attract *every* eligible man's attention. Ignoble as the evening's beginning had been, that did not mean the rest of the night must be to no purpose. Lucy would dedicate herself to Queen Charlotte's scheme, now that she was in the thick of it.

Not that the evening's success was entirely up to her, she amended with a small frown and a sideways glance at Lord Oxenby. If he chose to be tight-lipped, recalcitrant, or just plain unpleasant, it would make it all the more difficult for Lucy to shine. Which meant that she would have to make an effort at coaxing a good mood out of Lord Oxenby despite their mutual confinement to each other for the entire evening.

Others had joined in the dancing by now, and the music was winding toward a closing. Lucy fished around in her mind for a subject that might engage his interest or at least smooth over this rough moment. She toyed with the idea of asking after his costume, but Reuben had already explained that Oxenby was dressed as Cock Robin. What was there to say about Cock Robin? How likely was a deep, philosophical treatise on who might have shot the arrow into the red breast of the poor creature of lore? For that matter, her own troubadour's costume provided no fodder for conversation either.

So the topic that always served to secure conversation with her papa's guests and put them in a relaxed mood must do. "Lord Oxenby, your estate is in Essex, is it not?"

He scowled just a little as he made his bow and she her curtsy, and she could easily guess he wondered why she asked. After a moment he nodded and offered a mumbled, "Yes."

"I have spent far too little time in Essex," she said as he led her off the dance floor, "and know too little about it. Tell me your impressions."

"Of Essex?" he inquired still scowling.

"And your estate," she urged.

His scowl only deepened, and she could not help but notice that his scar puckered a little near his eye when he frowned so. Then suddenly a look of understanding dawned across his features. It relieved the scowl, but left a rather unpleasant, cynical smile in its wake. "Ah, I see. We are to make agreeable conversation."

Now it was Lucy's turn to scowl. Really, he was the most ill-tempered fellow, taking umbrage at the most rudimentary efforts at civility. "Is there anything wrong with making agreeable conversation?" she snapped.

"Wrong with it? No. It is merely that you and I have never managed it before."

She had a strong urge to reach up and slap that odious little smile from his mouth, but it would never serve the evening's purpose. Besides, she was loathe to touch his face, because it might remind him that she had once said something unfortunate about his scar, and she did not care to suffer his censure on that matter yet again.

Her hand remained in his, from his having led her from the dance floor, but now she pulled it free as she gave him a cold glance. "If we've never managed to be civil before, whose fault is that?"

Lord Oxenby's lips parted, but no sound came forth. She waited for his inevitably scathing rejoinder, but it was not forthcoming. It was another moment's pause before Lucy realized that she had literally stunned him with her question. He glared down at her, wordless.

She pressed her lips together, utterly confounded by the man. Had he forgotten that *he* had been the one to take everlasting umbrage? Had he ceased to recall that any subsequent show of friendliness on her part had ever been met with a cold, distancing gaze from him?

"Oh, for pity's sake," Lucy said now, even as that cold gaze began to resurface in his eyes. "We hate each other. Fine. Very well. So be it," she declared, tossing her head in agitation. She swallowed down the feeling, raising her gaze squarely once more to meet his. "But for one night can we not agree to pretend otherwise? Please, Lord Oxenby? For Godmama's sake?"

Oxenby stared again, but a new emotion had risen in his gaze. "I am astonished," he said, the words matching his expression. "The superior Lady Lucianne has used the word 'please' to me."

Lucy's own gaze narrowed in response. "It is a politeness, sir," she said coolly. "But you would be unfamiliar with such a thing as simple politeness, so I forgive your ignorance."

She expected the chill to return to his eyes, but now it was her turn to be astonished, for he laughed. It was a short sound, seemingly reluctant, but all the same it warmed his expression and caused her to stare at him.

"Ouch," he said, putting a hand to his heart. "That dagger hit true. I *am* being impolite. I beg your pardon, Lady Lucianne, and am utterly sincere in my apology even if you won't believe it."

"I will pretend to believe it, my lord, if you will pretend to act the part of gentleman and allow us to get through this night without unnecessary incivility."

He bowed his head, a courtly gesture that caught at her, made her abruptly see a hint of the charm that others had always claimed the man possessed, but which she'd not witnessed in years. "It is an agreement," he said.

"Well then," she said, taken aback. She gave a short nod, and said again, "Well then! Good."

They stared at each other, and Lucy wondered if he felt as suddenly at a loss as she did. They'd been at odds for so long, a truce was an unknown commodity between them. She had no idea how to go on, for he was abruptly, at least for tonight, not her enemy—but neither was he her friend.

The musicians struck up a new tune, unknowingly providing a release from the awkward moment. Without a word or a hesitation, Lord Oxenby extended his hand to Lucy. She accepted it and stepped forward, to dance once more at his side, only belatedly remembering to paste a smile upon her lips. At least this time they did not promenade by themselves for the first half of the dance as they had before.

They did not speak as they danced, but she was aware of a change in his demeanor all the same. Their first dance had been a stiff affair, accentuating the difficulty Reuben had told her Lord Oxenby had with his leg, but this second dance was a different thing. Now he moved with better grace, and he bestirred himself to cast smiles at the crowd, exchanging nods with the onlookers and other dancers. Taking her cue from him, she did the same.

There was to be a pause between the second and third dances, in order that the musicians and dancers alike might refresh themselves. It was impossible to ignore the gimlet eye of the queen as soon as this pause manifested itself, so Lord Oxenby led Lucy to the queen's side.

"Oxenby," she said at once, her expression not quite neutral, "you may be the Lord of the Masquerade, but that still gives you no right to monopolize a girl's time. You are to find another partner for the next few dances. You must share yourself a bit with others tonight," she said dismissively, her attention already shifting to Lucy.

Lucy glanced quickly up at Lord Oxenby from under her lashes, faintly mortified by the queen's direct manner, but if Lord Oxenby minded the queen's dismissal of him from Lucy's side, it did not show. But why should he mind? If anything, he would be relieved. Did he realize that the queen meant to parade Lucy before a selection of eligible men? Did everyone realize it? How could they not? Was it not terribly, awfully clear?

Lucy felt color flood her cheeks, but just then her gaze met Lord Oxenby's. She expected to find faint humor there, at her expense, or worse yet pity, but instead she saw something she'd not seen in his gaze since they were younger. It was a kind of understanding, a sort of commiseration. Oh yes, he realized the queen was not above using the moment to promote her goddaughter—but there was a further understanding there, too. It was not exactly pity . . . it was more like *discernment*.

Of course, he *had* to know what it was to be stared at, to be singled out in a crowd. He'd spoken to Reuben a few times about the burden of being scarred and having to work to keep his gait from becoming a limp, of having some gazes averted while other gazes fixed upon his obvious flaw. Lucy knew through her brother something of this man's hurt, and now looking into his eyes she saw something of it for herself. He did not pity her, not exactly, but she thought perhaps he also did not envy her the position she must hold tonight, a puppet to the queen's bidding.

He turned away, which ought to have been a relief, but instead Lucy felt strangely bereft when their mutual gaze was broken.

"Lucianne!" the queen snapped, her tone making it evident that Lucy had not been paying her heed.

"Ma'am?" Lucy asked at once.

"I asked you to play us a tune on that piccolo of yours," Queen Charlotte said, settling back in her chair in clear expectation that her command would be met.

Lucy reached down to the little pouch that hung at her hip, pulling forth the piccolo.

"The gentleman who offers the most gracious compliment on your playing shall be the lucky one to next dance with you," the queen pronounced. "I shall be the judge."

Lucy felt her mouth go dry—*the very idea*! She'd heard of playing for one's supper . . . but playing for a dance partner? She knew the queen's game was to make her the center of the entire evening, but that did not stop each new contrivance from being a small and torturously embarrassing consequence.

Still, she played a little melody, inexpertly rendered because her mouth had gone dry. One would have thought it the finest piece of music, however, to judge from the effusive compliments offered by a half dozen gentlemen.

"Could we but drink sound, that would have been as ambrosia to our ears," assessed a twinkly-eyed Lord Heath, whom Lucy hoped would win the dance since he was a family friend. They had danced together before.

"I shall cover my ears that I may never hear another note of music, so sweet was your offering," said one Captain Wymer.

His compliment was deemed by the queen as the winner.

Captain Wymer extended his hand to Lucy at once, for the third set of dancers was just beginning to assemble. She took it with a suppressed sigh. *Silly goose,* she silently chided herself at once, *how is this different than your first season?* She'd been eager enough then to be seen, to be sought out, to be courted by many beaux, the better to choose among them. No one but she and the queen knew how planned this event was, how deliberate. She'd be an utter fool not to take advantage of the occasion.

She lifted her chin, smiled at the attractive Captain Wymer, and hoped her new slippers were up to an entire evening of dancing.

Reuben grunted, an unhappy sound, causing Victor to glance in the same direction as his friend. Reuben's sister lingered with her fourth dance partner, chatting easily with the man. Like himself, she had been required to dance every dance, their status as Lord and Lady of the Masquerade forcing them to the utmost in social duty. At least she looked as if she were enjoying her present gentleman's company—in fact, Victor realized with faint surprise, despite a leg that was already beginning to ache a bit, he was enjoying himself as well. There were worse things in life than to have one's company sought after.

He echoed his friend's grunt, but this was for his own slow-topped ways, for it struck him that while the queen was not above promoting Lady Lucianne, he was not above promoting himself. It was why he'd first come to London years earlier, to fulfill his father's wish that the Oxenby name be established among the highest-flying families in the realm. The perfect opportunity had fallen at his feet and, until this moment, he'd been insensible to it.

So if Lady Lucianne could enjoy herself this evening, Victor would be a fool not to follow her example.

It was not Reuben's sister who caught Victor's eye now, however, but the man entering the hall just beyond where she curtsied to her latest partner. The man entering was none other than Reuben's own father.

"I see Lord Dorcaster is here," Victor said at Reuben's side.

"Papa?" Reuben said, his frown deepening.

"Did you expect to see him here tonight?"

Reuben shook his head, his mouth thinning from uneasiness. "He . . . he has not been much of one for social events of late."

They both watched as Lord Dorcaster stumbled forward, just managing to collect his balance and save himself from a fall.

"Good gad, he is half-seas over!" Reuben stated grimly.

The horrified expression that dawned on the face of the queen's majordomo revealed he'd belatedly realized what Reuben had—that he'd admitted a drunken man to the queen's assembly.

"It is not like your father to indulge," Victor noted quietly.

"Lately it is." Reuben cast his friend a quick glance. "I learned something recently, Victor."

"Oh, gad, no," Victor said at once, knowing what Reuben would reveal even before he could say it, as it was a worry they'd both shared before. "He invested too heavily. Just as you feared," he suggested darkly.

"Every penny he could lay hands on. He called in old debts. He's refused to hand over Mama's monthly pin money. He hasn't paid our steward in three months. He hasn't paid his tailor in a sixmonth—"

"I never should have mentioned that damned silver mine."

"It was making him money," Reuben said. He tried to shrug, but the gesture was forced. "He wanted to make more." He shook his head at his father's folly.

"You take risks with your surplus, not from your essentials."

Reuben shook his head again and made a disgusted noise of agreement. "He's come looking for me. He's clearly distressed," he said grimly, watching as his father shrugged the majordomo and a footman's hands from either sleeve.

Victor lifted his chin, bracing himself for the news that Lord Dorcaster obviously carried with him. "I haven't heard a thing from my man in New Holland, but I also have not sorted through today's post. A letter could have arrived." A letter from the New Holland silver mine in which he and Lord Dorcaster had both invested—apparently Lord Dorcaster more heavily than he ought to have done.

"The last letter I saw said there were signs of depletion," Reuben said hollowly.

Victor took a deep breath, letting it out slowly, his silence confirming what Reuben had said. When he'd suggested investing in the mine to Lord Dorcaster, he'd been trying to help, to assist Dorcaster in rebuilding a dwindling family fortune. Reuben had been enthused at first, too, but his enthusiasm had waned as warning signs had appeared. But diminishing returns and cautious reports had not been enough, it seemed, for Lord Dorcaster. "Reuben—"

"No blame!" Reuben interrupted with a short, sharp gesture of his hand. "You are to take no blame on yourself. You gave him a chance, and he chose to be foolish, to risk more than he could afford."

"We don't know that he's had bad news."

Reuben glanced across the room, watching as his bleak-faced father struggled to appear sober, walking with an overly careful gait toward his son, a worried majordomo and footman in his wake. "Don't we?"

Then disaster struck, for Lady Lucianne approached her father.

They could not hear her words, but they saw Lord Dorcaster clasp both her hands and bury his face against them, his shoulders shaking. Reuben began to move, to interrupt before harm could be done, but neither he nor Victor had taken more than a few steps before they saw Lady Lucianne lose all color from her face.

"Damn him!" Reuben said under his breath, doubling his haste, with Victor moving as his shadow.

"Reuben?" Lady Lucianne asked, her voice shaking, as her brother stepped to her side. "Is it true? Papa says all our money is gone. We are penniless—?"

Reuben shook his head violently, silencing any further comments that others might overhear. "I don't know," he murmured shortly. "Let me talk with Papa."

"Of course," she said, the words half-lost under the moan Lord Dorcaster gave as he turned to his son.

"Reuben! We are sunk! Sunk, I tell you," Lord Dorcaster cried.

"Sunk into drink, clearly," Reuben said aloud. But under his breath he cautioned his father, "Hush now, Papa. Come with me."

Dorcaster nodded, momentarily satisfied, it would seem, by the simple fact of having found his son.

"Could you tend to Lucy's needs?" Reuben asked Victor, even as he took up his father's arm.

Victor nodded at once, smothering a sigh. Reuben had indicated that any financial concerns were being kept from his sisters—but the elder of the two had just been roughly made aware. Lady Lucianne had to be wondering exactly what Victor wondered: Was there a dowry for her? For her sister, Rebecca? How could there be if the family finances were "sunk"?

Never mind Victor was not the best-suited candidate to divert Lucianne's attention at that terrible moment, the task had fallen to him. From the corner of his eye he noted Reuben guiding his father out onto a balcony and presumably downstairs to the ground level and the gardens below. He also caught a glimpse of relief on the majordomo's face that the drunken lord's removal from the queen's presence had been secured.

Another glance showed that Lady Lucianne struggled to wipe a dark frown from her spritelike face.

"Perhaps it is not so bad as your father made it sound," he suggested quietly.

"I knew something was wrong. The servants have been complaining about their wages . . ." Lady Lucianne murmured, still staring at where her brother and father had disappeared into the gardens.

What a way to find out such ill news! Victor thought. Even the usually toplofty Lady Lucianne looked shaken. She might not welcome his hovering presence at her side, but for his friend's sake Victor meant to stay there, at least until Reuben made a reappearance.

"Who knows how long they'll be, my lady, or what word they'll have to give you then. Best to put on a brave face for now."

"Yes. Yes, of course," she agreed. She shook her head, as though to clear it of cobwebs.

"And smile," he advised.

She managed a small, crooked one.

Victor led her back to the queen's side, where that lady accepted a cup of punch from a masquerader dressed as a highwayman.

"Ah, Oxenby!" the queen greeted him from over her goblet of punch. "You are just in time to continue the festivities."

One diversion would serve as well as another, Victor supposed. "How may I be of assistance, Your Majesty?"

"I know you play the violin, and very prettily, too. You are to accompany Lady Lucianne on the piccolo, and everyone is to dance to your tune. Maestro Adolphino"—she waved toward the musical conductor—"has provided a violin for your use."

Victor inclined his head in acceptance of the task. "As you please, Your Majesty. Although I fear my execution may be poor for lack of practice."

"With no practice playing together, we both can only do our best, which of necessity must be humble," Lady Lucianne said.

Victor looked at her. It was a simple statement of truth, but a humbled comment was not what he normally expected from her. Haughtiness, yes—but humility? Or had she abruptly learned humility from the last five minutes' folly? Regardless of why she had said it, he could not deny that she was doing her best to play the pretty. It behooved him to live up to her example, whether or not it was sincere.

"We shall try to do our best. Is the tune determined?" Victor inquired, allowing none of his musings to creep into his tone.

"What would you care to play?" Lady Lucianne asked, surprising him again by not demanding they play a piece with which she was wholly comfortable—but she was most likely distracted by far weightier thoughts.

They settled on "May the Maids a-Milking Go," a tune familiar to them both that well suited a country dance. He attempted the beginning, but quickly determined that two feathers on his right sleeve must be pulled free in order that he might play the instrument properly. Once that was corrected, they began anew. The tune was a bit uneven at first, but then they found the rhythm of the piece together and played until two full passes of the dancers had been completed.

The dancers had started on a third pass when Lady Lucianne piped a sour note. She blushed and laughed at her own mistake, interrupting her playing and causing Victor to misfinger his part as well. He joined a brief smile to her laugh, played a quick ending to the piece, and bowed to a round of applause to which Lady Lucianne also curtsied. She seemed to have recovered some of her equilibrium—and playing music together had been oddly . . . satisfying.

"I would say well done, my dears, but such dishonesty would only make you both laugh again," the queen assessed, a comment that made everyone else laugh as Lady Lucianne blushed again.

"What now, Lord of the Masquerade?" demanded the queen in a loud voice that belied she was in her seventieth year.

"Your Majesty, I see no reason why Lady Lucianne and I should be made to suffer alone," Victor replied at once. "Since we were made to display before the crowd our talents, or lack thereof, I believe it is only fair that the crowd should now have to perform for *our* benefit."

The queen clapped her hands together, perhaps more of a regal decree than a display of enthusiasm, but the gesture sealed the matter. "And who shall go first? Lord Daniels has a keen skill at the pianoforte—" Queen Charlotte began to suggest.

"Indeed he does, but I think our first performer must be yourself," Lady Lucianne said, taking the suggestion right out of Victor's mouth. He'd meant to compliment the queen, an avid and practiced player of the pianoforte, with the very same insistence. He glanced briefly at Lady Lucianne. It was . . . disconcerting to find they could work together in this unspoken fashion. They'd been at odds with each other for so long it was peculiar to be in step, however accidentally.

Years ago they had been less austere with each other than they were now, but he'd be wrong to put any oddness of form down to anything but the rarity of the evening, the public performance, the demand that they appear cordial. Of course he would, and he'd do well to remember that.

Queen Charlotte pretended to be unwilling, claiming her hands ached too much to play anymore, but it was not long before she had replaced the musician at his pianoforte and was filling the South Drawing Room with music.

Applause resounded at the conclusion of her performance, causing the queen to blush with pleasure. "Enough of that!" she exclaimed brusquely. "Who shall entertain us next?"

Lord Daniels, dressed as gypsy, conceded to a performance with an incline of his bald head that made his false gold earring fall off. A dozen others were then swiftly persuaded to volunteer their musical gifts for the queen's pleasure.

It took Victor only a few moments to conceive that, as Lord of the Masquerade, he could hardly slip away into the crowd, but must instead observe each and every performance. Even without that restriction, he meant to remain where Lady Lucianne was, which would be at the center of things. He leaned into the pianoforte just a little, to take the weight off his injured leg, and wondered how much it would ache tomorrow if he must dance and stand on it for unrelieved hours tonight? He allowed a sigh to escape him at the thought, but just then a small hand touched his sleeve.

It was Lady Lucianne, who silently nodded to three chairs being placed by footmen near the musicians. Had she ordered them brought forward? Or had the queen? Either way, fortunately Queen Charlotte chose to sit in the center one, leaving Victor and Lady Lucianne free to take a seat as well on either side of her. Victor sighed again, this time in relief.

The performances went on for over an hour—making Victor doubly glad chairs had been provided—and would have continued on if not for the approaching hour of midnight.

"Five minutes until masks are removed!" bellowed the majordomo from his guardianlike position near the door closest to the stairs.

"Everyone wearing a mask must stand at the center of the room," Queen Charlotte declared, rising from her chair to follow her own dictate.

Victor cast a quick glance at Lady Lucianne, even though he knew she also wore no mask, which was all to the good. The tradition of exchanging kisses with other revelers upon removal of one's mask need not apply to those who had none. They were free to straggle at the edges of the revelers, commending those souls who had been dressed more in the spirit of a masquerade.

Mixed with his relief, however, was a tickle of curiosity. How would the delicate Lady Lucianne have responded had she been made to reach up and kiss his scarred face, he thought in dark humor. Would their present unspoken truce have survived the trial? Would she recoil from the scar she'd once denigrated?

At that image, any fleeting amusement left him, and he had to work at keeping a frown from forming.

He looked on as the stroke of midnight was counted down by the crowd, watched as masks were drawn off, revealing few surprises. In fact, Victor's only real surprise came when he glanced once again at Lady Lucianne, who had gone pale as newly spun linen. Her eyes were wide, her elf's mouth shaped into an O, and her gaze fixed across the room.

Victor followed her gaze, afraid her father had returned to the room. But Lord Dorcaster was not to be seen. It was a late reveler who had just been admitted that had captured the lady's attention. The man she stared at had given up his colors, his military uniform now replaced by well-cut court clothes under a simple costume of wig and cape.

"Jerome!" Lady Lucianne whispered ever so faintly, but Victor had not needed to hear the words to know the man's identity. He was Mr. Jerome Holden, the lady's former fiancé.

Chapter 4

Jerome Holden, here? Lucianne had heard a whisper that he'd sold his commission, but when he'd not appeared in London along with the news, she'd assumed he'd gone to his family's country estate. Ex-soldiers were wont to go home . . .

But she ought to have known better. Jerome seldom did what other people were wont to do. What he wore tonight was a perfect example. Everyone else was in full costume, but he had chosen to appear in the usual court dress of dark coat and breeches over white silk stockings, his only nod toward costuming being a wig and cape to make him look vaguely like a barrister. But even those tokens were dispensed of the moment he'd made his bow to the queen, both wig and cape being handed off to the nearest footman.

How like him to bow only temporarily to the evening's dictates. Everyone said it was part of Jerome Holden's charm that he was unlikely to follow others' lead, that a great deal of the pull of his personality came from being spontaneous and unpredictable. Until just a few weeks ago, Lucianne would have agreed.

She cast her godmother a quick glance while trying to keep despair from overtaking her features. The queen would not have wanted to offend Jerome's father, the Viscount Broadwater, by not extending an invitation to a family possessing such an old and honored name. The queen could hardly be faulted for choosing good manners over her goddaughter's comfort—but Lucianne wished she had all the same. Tonight of all nights, when Papa had sobbed into her hands and mumbled frightening words of loss and debt and monies gone . . .

For that matter, where was Reuben? If he'd been in sight, Lucy had no doubt she'd have taken refuge at his side, perhaps asking him to take her home even though it would mean abandoning Godmama's efforts on her behalf. But Reuben and Papa were not in the room, and it was entirely possible that Reuben had called for the carriage to take Papa home, meaning to return for his sister once Papa was abed. Their father had been foxed, clearly, and presumably devastated by financial woes she could only imagine. Bed was the best place for him. At any rate, Reuben was not at hand.

Unfortunately, Jerome Holden was.

She'd not seen or spoken with Jerome since their quarrel that day in Hyde Park, when he had leaped down from his own carriage and abandoned her there. He'd gone directly back to his regiment, forgoing the remainder of his leave, and never deigned to respond to her letter of apology for the spectacle they'd made.

He *had* to know she would be there tonight, Lucianne acknowledged grimly. He would know that Queen Charlotte would be unlikely to throw an affair that did not involve her now unbetrothed goddaughter. He had come on purpose, no doubt to demonstrate that the disgrace of that park scene no longer touched him.

Once she would have trusted him not to shift the

weight of that disgrace onto her—but now she was not so sure. He'd surely be a gentleman. But would he be a gentleman only on the outside—sweet of manner, but cruel by deed? He had a honeyed tongue, one that could make you question your interpretation of events, could make you doubt what you'd seen or heard, could make you wonder if you'd been wrongheaded all along. That had been why she'd lost her temper so disastrously with him two weeks past, because she'd finally felt so baffled by his banter, so uncertain of his intended meaning, that she'd demanded stridently that he explain himself.

"Explain myself? Whatever do you mean?" he'd said a fortnight and two days earlier in the middle of Hyde Park. There had been a glimmer of amusement, as ever, in his eyes.

She'd pursed her lips, and thought to lower her tone, which had been steadily climbing. "I am asking for a serious conversation, Jerome," she said with a small blush, for the use of Christian names had only been agreed to quite recently, a privilege brought about by the length of their engagement. "Jerome, you know I very much enjoy your sense of humor, but at the moment it feels rather patronizing. I want to—"

"Patronizing, Elf? Such a big word." He rolled his eyes with exaggeration, making it obvious he knew his words could only serve to goad her.

"Now, that is exactly what I mean! I wish to speak soberly with you and you make sport at my expense—"

"It's not at your expense, Elf. And if the sober part bothers you, we can rectify that by going to a pub I know just two blocks from the park."

"I meant sober as in serious," she said pointedly.

He wrinkled his nose. "Serious? God forfend, we have no need to be serious."

"*I* do. I want to talk to you about our wedding breakfast."

"I suggest we hold it in the morning."

Lucianne did smile ever so slightly at that, for his frivolous quips were half his charm, and the playful thing he did with his eyebrows dancing that left some girls in rapture.

"Jerome," she said, shaking her head and with an effort resuming an earnest expression, "I need you to agree to some things, important things. Your leave will be over in a few days, and so many decisions are difficult to make by post. Such as where the breakfast is to be held, and do you wish there to be cake afterward, and will lemonade suffice or ought we to have several wines?"

"No whining, Elf. Such wailing and weeping gives me a headache."

She glowered at him. "*Wine,* as of the grape."

"Ah, Bacchus's gift to mankind! Fruit of the vine. The poets' nectar. 'Drink thy wine with a merry heart'—"

"So then, we are agreed. There shall be several courses of wine," Lucianne interrupted, raising her tone once more in order to override his. "But where will we host the breakfast?"

"Anywhere will do. You decide, Elf."

At least he'd given her a direct reply, if not any actual assistance. Lucianne took a deep breath, let it out, and ignored that his use of her brother's nickname for her was particularly vexing today. She was a woman grown, about to marry, not some childlike creature to be humored. Perhaps it was time to insist the nickname be revoked? she thought.

"My aunt—"

"Your mother's aunt? The ancient creature who bemoans that dresses have lost the use of panniers?" Jerome asked, making a face as he picked up the reins of his curricle.

"No, let us not move just yet! I would rather your attention not be divided with your driving," Lucianne said hastily, putting a restraining hand over his. When he complied, she quickly gathered her train of thought. "But, yes, that is the aunt I meant, Aunt Eustace. She has a town house here in London that is large enough to include a ballroom. It is not in the best part of town, I fear, although it is still respectable enough. She has offered to allow us to—"

Jerome wrinkled his nose at her again. "But if we have it there, then she'll expect to be at table, will she not?"

"Of course."

He shook his head. "She's too old."

Lucianne folded her hands together in her lap, taken aback. "Too old to sit at breakfast?"

He nodded. "Exactly. She would look odd."

"Odd? Or just merely old?"

"Are they not the same thing?" He flashed her another grin.

Lucianne took another steadying breath and began to shake her head. "She *is* my aunt, and she would be doing us a favor—"

"No, we'll have to find somewhere else."

Lucianne sat back against the seat, struggling to tamp down her growing feeling of vexation. "Then *you* suggest someplace else."

"No. Don't want to. Can't make me." He did not stick out his tongue at her, but the gesture was in his tone.

"Jerome!" she said on a shaky laugh, one that had

less amusement in it than he might suppose and much more of a growing exasperation. "I am asking for your help here."

"You decide."

"I already have decided a great many things, such as which of our two parishes to marry in, and how many guests we ought to invite to the breakfast, and, for that matter, what day we'll marry on."

"Which is?"

"Jerome! I've told you a half dozen times it is to be April fourteenth."

"April fourteenth? No, that won't do. I'll still be with my regiment."

"But you said you would request another leave that week!" His regiment was one of the happy few positioned in Brighton, against the fear of a French naval assault along the southern coast, a mere eight-hour carriage drive from London.

"They don't give out leaves for every little thing, you know."

"It is not a little thing to be getting married."

"The army could care tuppence about people getting married."

Lucianne heaved a sigh. "Two days? Could you get permission to come to London for a mere two days?"

He shook his head. "Why don't we wait?"

Lucianne leaped to her feet, making the curricle rock. Heads turned their way. "Wait? But the fourteenth is less than a month away! A dozen plans have been made. The vicar, the church—"

"Zounds, woman, are you trying to spook my horses?" Jerome frowned at her, glancing not at his horses but at the tide of faces now observing their interaction.

"I am *trying* to have a conversation!" Lucianne

cried, aware her voice had risen and her tone had become strident. He would expect her to calm herself, as she had in the past, but she had no desire to smooth the moment over.

Jerome, however, seemed unaware of the warning nature of her reaction. "A wholly unnecessary conversation, I must point out," he hissed under his breath at her.

Lucianne clutched her skirt with both hands, a poor shadow of her sudden desire to throttle him. "I know," she ground out from between gritted teeth, "that men are generally uninterested in the details of the marriage ceremony, and I am even willing to now acknowledge that all of the decisions appear to be mine to make. I will comply and therefore bother you no longer with questions. I might even be persuaded that the date is to be changed. But, Jerome, it is no longer the wedding plans, or lack of them, which has me so agitated."

"Sit down." He reached up a hand even as he glanced around again at the many staring onlookers.

"I will not sit down. Not until you *listen* to me!" Lucianne's voice rose higher. "Don't you care that I'm agitated? Don't you want to know *why*?"

"You *will* sit down this instant, or else I will leave," Jerome countered. "I will not be spoken to in this manner."

"Nor will I!" Lucianne had all but howled, and that had been the beginning of the end of their betrothal.

Give Mr. Jerome Holden his due: He'd been true to his word. He'd stared at her, said not a word more, and exited the curricle, walking away from her across the park. She'd had to drive the curricle home herself, sending it back to him via one of her father's grooms. Except for her subsequent letter of apology, they had not exchanged a single word in the sixteen days since.

The curious part of it all was that *he'd* not been the one criticized for abandoning both her and his horses like that. Somehow all the blame had fallen on Lucy's shoulders—even Mama had timidly suggested that Lucy's public show of temper might have caused Mr. Holden such an agony of embarrassment that he'd quite forgotten himself.

Now there he was, at the masquerade meant to revive the reputation Lucianne had shattered with fishwifelike shrieks in the park. He'd gone back to his regiment, only to quit it almost before he could rejoin it—and tonight of all nights he had come to make his re-entry into civilian society.

She ought to have expected this, she thought grimly, for it was in perfect keeping with the rest of the evening's disasters: Godmama's making her Lady of the Masquerade; the unfortunate selection of Lord Oxenby as her Lord; not to mention Papa's alarming claims of financial ruin. Now that her former fiancé had made an appearance on this most awful of evenings, what was left to go wrong?

My dress could catch fire, she supposed to herself, half expecting it to spontaneously erupt in flames.

"Does the maiden wish to be rescued?" said a voice near her ear, making her jump. She twisted to find it was Lord Oxenby. He looked a bit foolish in his Cock Robin feathers and red waistcoat and yellow stockings, at least compared with Jerome's dashing court attire.

"I beg your pardon?"

"Your former fiancé is here. I wondered if you wished to share any of his company, or desired none of it? I can arrange it so you have either." His look was hooded, revealing nothing of his own opinion in the matter.

Never mind Oxenby's presumption—albeit an entirely correct presumption— that Jerome's presence might be disturbing to her. What *did* she want? Part of her wanted to deny that seeing Jerome again might be disquieting in any way, but a quick glance that revealed the man in question was decidedly striding in her direction convinced her otherwise.

"Lord Oxenby, I feel a terrible need for fresh air," she murmured quickly.

To Oxenby's credit, he neither smiled nor questioned her, instead instantly offering her his arm and leading her away at a smooth if somewhat hasty pace.

He led her out to a balcony, not the one Reuben and her papa had used, and down the stairs leading to the garden behind the house. There were no lights there, only that of a half-moon and some little light spilling forth from the windows. Queen Charlotte and the king had long been, to put it kindly, thrifty; they'd seldom seen any reason to spend money on such frivolous things as fairy lights for the garden.

"Holden saw us leave, of course. He could easily join us here," Oxenby pointed out as he stepped from the bottom stair and turned to face Lucianne.

She took her hand from his arm and glanced out into the dark garden.

"It would destroy your reputation were we to venture out there to hide," he said.

"Only what is left of my reputation anyway," Lucianne agreed. She looked up through her lashes at her companion, wondering what he would make of the frank statement.

"Wait here," was all he said, moving at once from her side back into the house.

As she rubbed her arms against the deep chill of the March night, regretting the absence of a shawl or cloak, she heard the unmistakable sound of musicians tuning up to play. In short order Oxenby came once again across the balcony and down into the garden, giving her a nod. "Mr. Holden is presently occupied conversing with the queen, after which he is committed to dance with Miss Gleason."

"I see," Lucianne said, and wondered if he could see through the gloom to the blush that spread on her cheeks. Somehow he'd maneuvered Jerome into a couple of obligations that would keep him from her side for a while. It made her feel . . . odd that he'd gone to such bother on her behalf. They might have agreed to be pleasant for the evening, but pleasant did not necessarily include having to waylay former fiancés.

She lifted her chin, silently denying the confusion and vulnerability that Jerome's presence had brought over her. "I must wear my heart on my sleeve, for you to know Mr. Holden's arrival was . . . awkward for me."

"Hardly. It was the kind of moment that would be awkward for anyone."

"Oh, yes, I see. Of course." She felt her blush deepen. She'd put his actions down to an unexpected gallantry, but it had been only simple deduction on his part.

No, that was not true, she thought. Simple deduction would have given him the information, but not the impetus to act on it. He'd done her a favor, whatever his motivation, and he deserved her thanks. She parted her lips to offer as much, but he interrupted.

"Come this way," he said, already beginning to move. She thought he meant to offer her his arm once more, but instead he took up her hand and pulled her forward with him.

The light behind them retreated, leaving them only the moon's timid glow as they entered the garden. "Where are we going?" she squeaked.

"Back in the house, by way of another door," his voice floated back to assure her. "We can't stay out here—we'd freeze."

She clung to his hand, unsettled by their sudden flight even while she was soothed by his aplomb in an odd situation.

It took only a few moments to make their half-blind way to another entrance, this one opening to reveal a startled guard who stared wide-eyed at the costumed intruders.

"All these doors look the same from the garden," Oxenby said good-naturedly to the guard. "My good man, can you lead us to the stairs?"

The perturbed guard was more than happy to return them to the majordomo's dominion just outside the South Drawing Room. Lucy moved toward the threshold, but Oxenby pulled her back from entering. He led her aside in the corridor, still in sight of other attendees who moved in and out of the room, but where only she could hear his voice.

"Your reputation is safe here, and it will take Mr. Holden some time to learn where you've gone. However, I think I must point out that you probably cannot avoid his company all night if you remain at the masquerade and he should choose to insist upon speaking with you."

"And I cannot leave for home. Godmama would never forgive me for abandoning my role as Lady of the Masquerade." He might have replied, but she put her hand on his arm. "I feel a perfect fool for having been shaken for a moment, but you should know I am quite all right now. Mr. Holden and I were bound to encounter each other again—I just had not expected it tonight."

She hesitated, then withdrew her hand, for it suddenly seemed too intimate a gesture to have reached out and touched his sleeve even if it was randomly trimmed with feathers. "I thank you," she added, hoping her sincerity overrode any awkwardness there might be in her tone.

He stood close enough that she knew there was something behind his calm gaze, but she could only guess what it might be. Satisfaction with his own behavior? Appreciation that she'd been less caustic toward him than on other occasions? Whatever it was, it caused a shiver to course through her as he said simply, "You're welcome."

"What now?" she asked, as much to cover a suddenly awkward moment as to gain the information. She tore her gaze from his, pretending to observe the others who strolled or stood in the corridor.

"I would suggest we carry on as we were doing before."

"As Lord and Lady?"

"Exactly. Do you have any notions to add to the festivities?"

"Not a one."

He gave her a dry look. "Start thinking. I have some ideas, but they are not unlimited, and I would rather be occupied than not. It will make the evening more of a success."

And make the evening fly by faster, she mused, only to be half ashamed of the thought. She could hardly blame him for wanting to be free of her company. At least he'd been courteous enough not to say the obvious. She shook her head, not sure what to make of these peculiar new impressions of Lord Oxenby's character, which until tonight had been consistently cold, even harsh toward her.

"Are you ready to go back to our duties?" he asked, offering her his arm.

She nodded. "What is it to be now?"

"Chess."

"Chess?" she echoed, puzzled. Most of the party were unlikely to be interested in the game, even if a number of boards could be found.

"With human-sized pieces."

"Ah," she said, not entirely surprised to feel a grin spread across her lips, one that echoed his own.

Chapter 5

The "Knight" moved two steps forward and one to the right, as he'd been instructed to do.

Lord Oxenby, who was not one of the players but was acting as the officiator, announced, "Checkmate! White wins!" with a flourish of his hand.

Everyone broke into applause at the life-sized chess game's conclusion, even Queen Charlotte. The "Knight" (a military fellow whose infantry uniform had been deemed suited to the position) and all the other human-sized "pieces" relaxed from their stances to join in the applause. Princess Sophia, in her mermaid ensemble, had played the "White Queen," and looked quite pleased that white had won. Except for the princess, the "Knight" and one other fellow dressed as a priest who played a "Bishop," everyone else had placards hanging around their necks, on which was written the name of their position.

Despite the game's conclusion, Lord Wickam complained again of his status as a mere pawn, but Mrs. Ackerley told him to be grateful he'd not been eliminated in the first five minutes of play, as she had. Servants scurried to collect the placards and to pick up the lengths of rope that had been laid on the carpet in order to form the squares of the oversized board.

Lord Alvanley had been chosen the player for black, and Princess Esterhazy for white. They each now climbed down from the ladders that had been located and leaned against opposite walls in order to elevate them several rungs up, the better to see the layout of the board.

"Excellent play!" Lord Alvanley, the loser, said as he stepped down to the carpet.

"And yourself, sir," Princess Esterhazy said in an equally convivial tone. "Shades of the old French courts, eh, this idea of Oxenby's?"

"Quite," Alvanley agreed. "But enough of chess and my ignominious loss. Oxenby, what are we to do now?"

All heads turned to Lord Oxenby in expectation. One man stepped forward to echo Lord Alvanley.

"Yes, Oxenby, what are we to do now?" Jerome Holden said.

He did not wait for an answer, however, stepping at once before Lucy. "My dear lady, it is my great pleasure to see you again," he said, taking up her hand to bow over it.

He lifted his head, his gaze meeting hers, and at once she felt a flurry of confusion, for his expression lacked the rebuke she had expected to be there. Indeed, there was a manner of warmth in his gaze, and nothing of the coldness she had imagined would mark their first re-encounter.

"Good evening, Mr. Holden," she said, hoping she sounded calm. She suddenly felt foolish in her multicolored troubadour's gown and little hat, but she pushed the feeling aside by telling herself that any feelings of foolishness were just from the shock of seeing him again. She'd wished to marry this man once, had imagined the joy to be had from residing together, coming to know each other better, and with luck having their appreciation of each other grow with the years.

She'd once intended to fall in love with him.

Love or no, they'd once had a plan to be together, and it had fallen apart, and she had regretted it time and again in the sixteen days since she'd last looked upon his face. A girl was a fool to throw away a good connection, a man worthy of partnership—and she had done it in such a low, common fashion. She'd called herself a sapskull a hundred times since—and yet now was flustered by the lack of the same reproach in Mr. Holden's gaze.

The moment was interrupted by continuing calls for Oxenby to suggest further merriment, and his subsequent glance down at Lucianne.

"Food?" she suggested in a murmur, the only thought to come to her in her fluster, no doubt because her stomach was tumbling.

Oxenby lifted both eyebrows in doubt, but he threw up his hands in a gesture that quieted the calls for more. "Gentlemen! Ladies! I thought I would be lauded and indulged as Lord of the Masquerade, not made into an overworked, exhausted slave."

There were chuckles, but otherwise his protest fell on unsympathetic ears as more voices urged him to announce another scheme for their entertainment.

"Exhausted? 'Tis scarcely half past one," someone complained from the rear of the gathered crowd. This comment was met with even more huzzahs and whistles, causing Oxenby to lift his hands again.

"There is to be no rest for the wicked, I see. Very well then, but might I suggest we retire for a light repast before we continue our festivities?"

Now all eyes pivoted to the queen, who was known to order dinners that, unwanted by her, would therefore never be consumed by anyone else either. The tantalizing scents of a readied meal had been drifting into the drawing room since shortly before midnight. It was a stomach-growling reminder that the queen seldom allowed gatherings at her home to go past the evening hour of nine and that the readied supper would most likely never be appreciated by the attendees. Lucy had always wondered why the food was prepared in the first place, since the queen so seldom wished its presentation—but such was the privilege of royalty.

The queen put her head on one side, her gaze narrowed upon Oxenby, but then she surprised everyone by nodding. "Very well. Let us dine," she pronounced. Her daughter, Princess Sophia, gave an audible gasp of surprise.

The queen led everyone to the dining room, with the princess following in her domineering mother's shadow, and Oxenby and Lucianne in their royal wakes as before.

Oxenby was waved to the seat at the queen's right, and Lucy supposed she would be placed to her left, except that position was given to the princess. Which meant the seat right of Oxenby was given to Lucy, who had expected she would not speak with him during dinner, not in a gauche manner across the table. Now they were to be dinner companions. Not that it mattered, except that she could not imagine what they might yet have to say to each other.

Not that any gaucherie on her part would have been noticed anyway, she soon thought, for the table that had quickly been assembled by startled servants was of no size to serve all the queen's guests. The meal itself was not elaborate, lacking the multitude of many removes that a formal affair would have had, but it was good and hearty fare, beef in its gravy, and capons, sole in wine sauce, peas with onions, and a plentitude of light, fluffy buns. Lucy found herself wondering if the usually ordered-but-uneaten food was used for tomorrow's meals, or if the servants usually reaped the reward of the queen's peculiar habit. Either way, she doubted it went to waste, as the queen would abhor that more than she seemed to mind presenting an evening's repast.

Many of the gathering were forced to stand as they nibbled from plates balanced on their hands, looking all the more fantastic in their variety of costumes for having been crowded together into the moderately sized dining room.

The conversation quickly grew to a roar. Lucy had to all but shout at the gentleman, Lord Fairley, on her right, and so many people sought Oxenby's attention, she need not have wondered what they might speak about for she was not to have the chance. The only conversation they shared was Oxenby's half-shouted "I say, these buns are good. I think they added anise as well as currants," and Lucy's reply of "Godmama has a fondness for anise." But then Oxenby's attention was stolen away by a woman in some kind of Far Eastern costume who came to stand near to his left side.

Elbows bumped, wine spilled, and aside from an excess of warmth in the room, the guests gave every indication of enjoying the oddly informal repast.

Queen Charlotte, however, threw Lucy a speaking glance, one that clearly said that at best she was merely tolerating this turn of events, and all for Lucy's benefit. Instead of being cast down, Lucy had to stifle a sudden desire to giggle. It was no mean feat to get the queen of England to agree to feed so many, so late, but Oxenby had done it. He had charm, Lucy had to agree even to herself, even if it was for everyone else in the world but her.

But, she amended at once, that was no longer fair; he'd shown her something of the grace he lavished on others when he'd given her time to adjust to Jerome's unexpected presence, she had to admit. She began to understand why her brother liked the man. However, it was easy to like a charming companion. It was far more difficult to care for one who drips of censure and dislike. She must remember that Oxenby had long been more the latter with her than the former.

Lucy chewed her lip, lost to thoughts of character—and her Papa's character loomed, for she found she was quite capable of believing his claim of financial loss. There had been signs, enough that Lucy had been on the edgc of speaking of her concern to Reuben. She'd always had a dowry, she and Rebecca. Could they really be gone?

Someone slipped into the chair beside her, drawing her attention back to the moment: Jerome.

"Lucianne," he said, leaning toward her so that she might catch the quiet word in the noisy room.

"Mr. Holden," she said cautiously in return.

"I'm sorry," he said. "For that row in the park. It was . . . well, it never should have happened."

Her eyes flew wide in astonishment. "I accept your apology," she said at once. "And I offer one of my own."

A smile spread across his face. "Wonderful!"

Warmth flowed through Lucy at this turn of events. She'd expected censure, even anger, from him, not apologies and the hope of a friendship restored.

"I never meant to lose my temper—" she began to add, but she was interrupted by the queen's coming to a stand, the decisive signal that the meal was over whether or not anyone else was done. All the chairs were scraped back or plates placed on the crowded tabletop, and when everyone was on their feet, Queen Charlotte led the crowd once again to the South Drawing Room.

She turned at once to Lord Oxenby. "Well then, Lord of the Masquerade?"

"Cards?" he proposed. "For a bit, in order that our meal may settle?"

The queen's nod sent the servants once more into a scramble as they scurried to assemble enough tables and chairs for those who agreed to play. An odd collection of game, tea, and sofa tables were pressed into service, being brought from various rooms throughout the house.

Lucy was seated at a table with Oxenby, the Princess Sophia, and the statesman Lord Melbourne, but most of her attention centered on Jerome, who had declined to play and had moved to stand behind her seat. She was keenly aware of his presence behind her, and she had difficulty concentrating on the first hand of cards.

She gasped and froze in place when Jerome put his hands on her shoulders. He did not speak to her, but rather to Lord Oxenby.

"Come on then, Oxenby, you've appropriated nearly every moment of our Lady of the Masquerade's attention." Clearly, since entering, Jerome had learned of the evening's designations. "It is someone else's turn to enjoy her company," he went on, with every evidence of a light air. "Mine! Give me your seat," he bid.

If Oxenby expected a reaction from Lucy when he locked his gaze to hers, all she was able to give him was a round-eyed stare. It was one thing for Jerome to seek forgiveness and apologies, but his apparently complete forgiveness astounded her.

It was all she could have hoped for, but it was also . . . peculiar . . . disproportionate. Did the man have no rancor? No shadow of resentment?

Oxenby shifted his gaze from Lucy to Holden. He gave a small shake of his head while keeping a soft smile on his mouth. "No, I think not. I have the privilege here, as Lord of the Masquerade, and I choose not to surrender the lady's company. How often do I have a captive companion, I ask you?"

"Exactly my point, sir," Jerome said, still in that friendly, even jovial tone. "The lady has been your captive most of the night and no doubt desires a respite from gazing constantly upon the one visage."

Color came into Oxenby's face, as though to emphasize the scar that all eyes now avoided gazing upon. Lucianne gasped, having seen Jerome's words strike like a barb, piercing the casual amusement Oxenby had held in his demeanor.

"Mr. Holden!" She half turned in her seat toward Jerome, making his hands fall away, and feeling more befuddled than ever. She'd just been pondering the man's lack of rancor, and then he had delivered this unkind blow.

"Besides," Jerome went on, "one should not keep a lady from the company of her fiancé."

Cards dropped from Lucy's hands as she finished twisting in her chair to stare up at Jerome.

"Former fiancé," Oxenby pointed out, his tone coolly level.

"Not if I have anything to say to the matter. Princess Sophia, Lord Melbourne, please excuse Lady Lucianne," he said, already reaching to take Lucy's hand. He pulled her to her feet, bowed to the table, and led her away almost before she could execute a quick flounce of a curtsy.

Lucy glanced back over her shoulder in time to see

Lord Oxenby's narrowed gaze replaced with the cold, set expression she was far more used to. She gave him a helpless look, but when he began to rise to his feet, Lucy shook her head. She had no idea what Jerome was about, but better to talk it out with him now, and leave the blameless Lord Oxenby out of it.

Oxenby slowly sat back down, staring a moment longer, but then he waved another woman into Lucy's seat at the card table. The woman's reward for agreeing to fill the space was a sudden flash of a smile, one that twisted the scar near his mouth, from Oxenby.

"Mr. Holden!" Lucy cried again, belatedly attempting to plant her feet and cease the forward dash into which he'd pulled her.

He stopped and turned at her resistance, glancing briefly at her face and then around for a refuge. "The corner will have to do," he proclaimed, pulling her to the empty angle of the room he'd indicated.

"Mr. Holden!" Lucy repeated, snatching her hand from his. "You must explain yourself."

He gave a little quirk of his head, rather as one does when inviting someone in on a joke. "Is it not clear? We had our little quarrel, and it served to clear the air, and I wish to go on as before."

"Go on—! Do you mean, to be affianced again?"

"Yes," he said, taking up her hand once more. He pressed it flat over his waistcoat at his heart, crossing both his palms over it. "You never really cried off, you know."

"Oh, but surely—! I mean to say, I wrote you an apology, and you never responded, and my friends were politely offering condolences on the end of our betrothal—" She stopped in midsentence, gazing intently up into his light brown eyes. "You cannot possibly think, after that scene in the park . . . And you returned to your regiment! Without a word to me. And you left me in your curricle, just left me there. What else was I to think but what everyone else thought? That it was over."

"What *I* thought, Lucianne—that we'd had a spat. People do, you know. Certainly married people have spats all the time. I was hurt, but I thought it was obvious it was a mere nothing, really, and that everything should be as it had been. I *had* to go back to my regiment eventually, so why not at once, while our tempers cooled?"

Lucy pulled her hand free of his, the thump-thump of his heart beneath her palm too intimate and . . . *unexpected* at such a juncture. She shook her head in confusion, pressed her fingers to her forehead, and shook her head again. "Mr. Holden, what are you saying to me?" she blurted out.

"I'm saying I wish to be betrothed to you once more. I am now free of my military obligation. We can marry at any time you desire."

Lucy's lips parted in astonishment, the word "marry" ringing in her ears. Just like that, all the order that had slipped from her life could so easily be restored—the very thought of it made her feel light-headed. Disgrace could be erased. Humiliation could be put down to nothing more than a lovers' spat. She could have the future she'd been planning since her second season. She could have her life back, as it had been.

Certainly, leaving her papa's home must relieve something of the financial woes there, she thought, perhaps making it possible for Rebecca to have a dowry . . . ?

Lucy looked at Jerome again, really looked at him, deep into his light brown eyes. How like him this was. Jerome, as unpredictable as ever! But why was she not casting herself into his arms, or at least nodding fervently and whispering yes—oh, yes?

She had to tell him, first, that it was highly probable her dowry no longer existed. That was the only honorable option, of course. She thought it might give him pause—were their roles reversed, it would her, for a woman must consider the welfare of any subsequent children. But it seemed to her that if a man could forgive a humiliating display in the park, he must find more of value in his beloved than merely her purse. Her heart ought to be dancing, ought to be swelling with delight that he'd been unable to stay angry with, or away from, her.

Why instead did her attention go to the thought that Jerome's coloring was a lighter version of Oxenby's, the one man's hair and eyes being the color of honey, the other's as rich and dark as treacle. If not for his large, jagged scar, Lord Oxenby would certainly be the more handsome of the two, yet most people would account Jerome the handsomer because his good looks remained unmarred.

Yet it was not really their appearances that tugged at her concern as she pondered this re-offer of marriage, but a sense of confusion. Jerome had come back into her life so abruptly, so forgivingly, acting as unpredictably as ever. He was a whirlwind, and he made her head spin.

"Do you love me?" She spoke this most important of questions in a near whisper. "Jerome, do you love me?"

"Indeed, dear lady."

She closed her eyes, but she was unable to keep a wrinkle of dismay from furrowing her brow.

"I am not passionate enough for you," Jerome correctly assessed, the words causing her eyes to fly open once more as he took up her hand again. "That is easily solved." He cleared his throat. "Lady Lucianne, my heart swells with love for you. Nothing will content me until you agree to marry me," he said, his tone deep but not carrying, meant for their quiet corner only.

Her ears were ringing, as if she'd taken a strong blow to the head. Jerome was asking her to marry him, declaring his love, and her strongest response was a ringing in her ears? There was relief . . . but where was the soaring heart, the gleeful thrill? She'd known it before, the first time he had asked her to marry him. Was that a once-in-a-lifetime flutter? Was she expecting too much? Was she considering the wrong feelings, the wrong information for this weighty decision?

"This is too much, too soon after . . ." she began. "I . . . I need time. I need to think—"

"Come now, Lucianne. Say yes. You know you want to," he coaxed, the familiar, teasing smile in his honey brown eyes.

"Do I?" She took a small step back from him. He was pressing her, and she suddenly did not wish to be pressed in this matter of marriage.

"We suit, do we not? And only think of how long it will take you to learn if another man suits you. You don't wish to be tarrying on the marriage mart for months—or even years—longer."

She frowned at him, not so much for the truth of his words, but for his bluntness in stating them. There was a new gleam in his eyes now, not one of amusement, but something keener, cooler; he was aware his words had possessed an edge. He'd *meant* to remind her of her tattered reputation, her disquieting need for a fourth season. He'd meant to remind her that he was a good catch.

She put up her chin. "Are you saying I ought to have you since no one else will have *me*?"

He gave a small laugh—she frowned more deeply at him for it—and shook his head. "I am not trying to insult you, my sweet lady. I am proposing."

"A very queer manner of proposal, to warn me I might end on the shelf."

"I never said that."

"You implied it."

"Well then, what if I did? You're a forthright girl. You are forever bidding me not to embroider my stories—although a bit of embroidery makes them ever so much more entertaining, you must agree. You certainly laughed at them. But, to my point, *can* you hope for a better offer than mine?"

She might have laughed for the sheer effrontery of the question, but this was Jerome Holden and it was a bit late to cavil at his flashes of raw candor now. So many women found his frank comments, coupled with his embroidered tales, uniquely charming—Lucy had often been charmed herself. To give an outraged objection to his bluntness now would have been playing both him and herself false.

"Well?" His doubt was displayed in the lift of his eyebrow. "*Please* do not try to tell me some drivel that you hope tonight's folly could mean the bachelor Oxenby will have you?"

She made a stuttering noise of protest at this sudden and foreign thought, too startled to form a more formal denial.

His gaze widened in shock, misinterpreting her inability to articulate. "Good God, Lucianne!" He gave a disgusted laugh. "What were you thinking? That your face and dowry can persuade the man to abandon the single life? I must admit he *would* be marrying above himself, a thing most to be desired. By him. But what of you, my lady?"

She'd been ready to correct his erroneous thinking, but now her fluster turned into exacerbation: This was going too far. Lord Oxenby was no part of this matter and ought not to be dragged into it, not to his disparagement.

"Is it clever," Jerome continued, "to settle for a mere upstart of a baron, a man who still smells of the shop, when you can have a viscount's son of the bluest blood?"

Her exacerbation dissolved into anger. "A viscount's *second* son," she said pointedly.

Her barb did not reach him. "A second son likely to *inherit,*" he corrected her.

Lucy pressed her lips together and shook her head at his cool nature. No, she thought, these calm assessments of his were more than cool, they bordered on icy. She felt a dawning sensation, as though seeing the man reborn, or at least stripped of his social façade. Could she really want to marry a man who could so nakedly project the death of his older brother? Never mind it was probably the truth, that Jerome's older brother was in fragile health with delicate lungs and a chronic cough. Never mind that Lucy herself had pondered the very real possibility that one day she might be the Viscountess Broadwater.

"You're offended," Jerome said softly, coaxingly.

Oh, give him his due, she mused, he was perceptive of any disapproval of him. He knew how to provoke a response and then how to retreat behind softer tones or half-apologies, she saw that now, for here he was doing it once more.

"You know me, Lucianne. You know I must stir the pot. But surely that only adds to the spice of it?

We spat, we spit, but it is only a bit of sport in the end."

He stopped a moment, to fix his gaze to hers, concentrating his charm upon her. She felt it tug at her, as it always had, and she braced herself for his inevitable tones of persuasion and reasonableness.

"We know how to go on with each other. Come, say you'll have me." He reached out for her, smiling with one side of his mouth when she took another step away from him. "Do not play the coquette, Lucianne, not now. Please give me my answer."

Still he charmed, still made her want to please him. But it was too late, she'd changed, or she'd seen a change in him, something to which she could no longer remain blind.

"No," she said, half amazed at how right the answer sounded. "No, I do not wish to marry you, Mr. Holden."

"What?" he said on a laugh. "Lucianne, heads are turning our way! Our moment alone is coming to an end. Let us not play at this game, not now—"

"You are correct. No games. I have a duty tonight I must complete for my godmother, so I ask that you please do not disturb or speak to me again this evening," she instructed softly. "Perhaps we can be friends in the future, but tonight that is not possible. I refuse your offer."

He scowled. "You're still angry about the scene in the park—"

She shook her head. "What does it matter? Our betrothal is not to be resumed."

"By God, you *do* mean to have the upstart, don't you?" he cried, and now there was nothing soft or coaxing in his tone. It rang out from their corner, turning heads and abruptly silencing other conversations.

"Holden, colorful as ever," interrupted a voice. "Might this conversation be moved to the garden?"

Lucy turned her head to confirm that it was Lord Oxenby who had come up behind her, his hands clasped behind his back in a casual pose that was not echoed in his eyes.

"Or perhaps put it to an end altogether?" Oxenby went on. "I have need of my Lady of the Masquerade's assistance, and must whisk her away from your side, Holden."

"That's her very hope!" Jerome said with a sneer.

"The garden?" Oxenby suggested again, a little more firmly.

Holden made no move, but seemed to become aware again of the crowd that gawked at them, and his visible anger slipped away. In its place formed the essence of indifference, an ennui threaded through both his posture and his accents.

"Or will it ruin your little scheme to have its target know of your intent?" he said silkily, directing his words to Lucianne. "That you hope to catch Oxenby in parsons' mousetrap? But, oh my, I think I have spoiled that surprise. So much for that hope now, eh, my lady?"

Lord Oxenby glanced between Lucy and Jerome, a puzzled question written across his face.

"She's set her cap at you," Jerome explained, then made a show of yawning. Others might see the display of unconcern as he meant it to be seen, but Lucy saw the dark flash of venom in Jerome's eyes.

Murmurs rippled through the crowd and fans snapped open in a pretense of hiding astonished expressions.

"Ahh," Oxenby said, glancing sideways toward Lucianne. The simple sound, inherit with hesitation and doubt, brought color to Lucy's cheeks where Jerome's many claims had not.

"Mr. Holden is quite mistaken—" she began to explain.

"Lucianne!" interrupted the queen, stepping into the fray.

Instant silence met her presence as she gazed somberly at each of them.

"My girl, you seem to have a surfeit of suitors," she said to Lucy, although it was at Lord Oxenby that she gazed intently.

"Never so, ma'am," Lucianne said very low.

The queen eyed her and harrumphed. "True! One can never have too many suitors," she declared.

Lucy might have explained she'd meant something else altogether, but she did not, painfully aware that she was once more firmly embroiled in a scandal. She feared that anything she might say would only make it worse. *So much for restoring my reputation. So much for putting scandal behind me. I'll become a burden to my family, just when my family could use every advantage. So then, no, I will retire to the country, live simply, take up watercolors and the sighting of birds and being Auntie to any children Rebecca might have . . .*

The queen was not done with her yet, though. "Lady Lucianne," Queen Charlotte said with regal authority, her German accent coming to the fore. "Mr. Holden and Lord Oxenby, the three of you, in my sitting room. At once!"

Chapter 6

"She refused my suit," Holden told the queen, looking bored where he lounged at her dressing table, her other brocade-covered sitting room chairs being occupied by the queen, Lady Lucianne, and Victor himself.

Victor glanced at Lady Lucianne, but her eyes were firmly on the carpet, every emotion hidden from his gaze except the dejection he could see in her slumped shoulders. She'd removed her jaunty little hat and cast it aside, revealing a plait of dark hair that had been coiled and pinned beneath it.

The queen, who had shooed out all her usual attendants and servants, turned to Lucianne. "Is this so, my girl?"

Now Lady Lucianne lifted her gaze from the carpet. "Yes, Godmama," she said, her tone unmistakably firm.

"And you do not wish to change your mind?"

"No, Godmama."

The queen sniffed, mumbled something in German under her breath, and gave a single wave of her hand. "You are dismissed, Mr. Holden," she declared, sparing him only a glance before turning her attention back to her goddaughter.

Holden made his bow to the queen, his face blandly set but his shoulders tense, presumably from aggravation rather than regret. "Your servant, ma'am," he murmured.

The room fell silent as he made his way out, but the moment the door was closed behind him, the queen spoke. "How are you to recover from this affair, Lucianne?" she demanded, her tone rife with exasperation.

"What do you mean, ma'am?" Lady Lucianne asked, but Victor suspected it was a rhetorical question, for there was a haunted quality in her eyes. She already knew everything the queen proceeded to recite back to her: her loss of aplomb in the most fashionable park in London; the ruined betrothal; the tainted fourth season. And now yet another public squabble with Holden, a man of some considerable social standing.

"*Bei Himmel,* Lucianne!" the queen scolded. "Usually it is the man whose reputation suffers when an engagement goes awry, not the female. I do not know how you ever manage to pull it onto your own head, but you have done it twice now! I honestly despair for your reputation."

Lady Lucianne lost any color that might have remained in her cheeks, but she put back her shoulders. "So then, we must all agree I am not destined for marriage," she said evenly. "For what use is a woman's reputation but to secure her a husband? I am to be a spinster. So be it. There are worse fates—"

The queen made a scoffing sound from between down-turned lips. "Not for an earl's daughter, there is not. Of course you will marry! It is simply a matter of how well."

That statement, Victor thought with an interior grimace, was truer than the queen could know. He had a note, tucked now in his coat pocket, that had been delivered to him while he'd played at cards, a note from Reuben. He could recite its simple message without a second glance:

Ox—It is as we feared with regard to Father. I've taken him home. We'll talk later. I rely upon you to bring L. home tonight.—R.

That note confirmed what Lady Lucianne was surely astute enough to have pondered: that her family had no money now for her dowry. He had not shown her the note. It contained no information of use to her this night, only hurt and harm—but the possibility of losing her dowry had to have been preying on her mind even while Holden had been asking once again for her hand.

Yet she had turned the man down.

Victor let his gaze wander over her where she sat, and wondered why. Acceptance would have solved so many difficulties for her, for her sister, and her family. Could it be she refused to believe her father's confession, putting it down to too much drink? No, she might be proud, but Lady Lucianne was neither foolish nor fatuous. She'd admitted the servants had been grumbling over not being paid regularly. She knew something had gone badly awry.

Could it be she had other hopes? There were plenty of men who would marry an earl's daughter—but those men came only in two types: titled men with no fortunes who hoped to pad their purses, or rich Cits with no titles who wished to marry above themselves.

Either was less than Lady Lucianne had been raised to expect. So why not choose Holden, the embodiment of whom her husband ought to be and how her life ought to unfold?

It struck him that, earl's daughter or no, it would be far more like her to choose the spinster's life than to compromise. It had to be, for some reason, that she'd not wanted to pledge herself to Holden for a lifetime.

Lady Lucianne was a shrewder woman than he'd ever given her credit for before, if that was the case. If she'd seen something in the man's demeanor that had dissuaded her from marrying him, then he had to think her intellect came before her pride.

Imagine that.

Before tonight he would not have felt a speck of pity for her situation, but before tonight he'd seldom glimpsed the more thoughtful side of her personality. Her brother loved her, which meant she had redeeming qualities even if she could only rarely be bothered to display them before Victor.

It flitted through his mind that, were he to act a better friend to Reuben, he would offer for Lady Lucianne. Her reputation would be saved, she'd have her married status and presumably all the joys of womanhood such as house, hearth, children.

He'd have a wife . . . and there the generosity of his spirit quailed, for having a wife was nothing like any other aspect in his life. Any wife, even a neglected wife in a far corner of the globe, was a force for change upon a man's life. A wife nearer to home, the sister of one's closest friend . . . such a wife could not be a casual influence.

No, he thought, offering for her was impossible. Honor had its limits.

The force of a weighted stare brought Victor's attention back to the moment, one glance into the queen's clever, calculating face telling him she'd had the same thought. His heart skipped a beat.

He shook his head.

She nodded hers.

"Me? Marriage?" He spoke directly to her.

She nodded again, a simple regal command even if it was unspoken.

This was too much. He'd been asked to be the queen's friend, but this went beyond that charge. "Your Majesty," he said, his heartbeat resumed and now pounding in his temples, "it is impossible. I understand why you seek this for the lady, but you've turned to the wrong deliverer. Only ask the lady herself."

Lady Lucianne glanced between the queen and Victor, clearly puzzled by his statement. "Marriage? I have said I will *not* have Mr. Holden, and I quite meant it."

The queen ignored her. "I *will* ask her, but not before you declare yourself, Oxenby. Say you would do it."

"Impossible," he repeated, shifting in his seat.

"Nonsense! It is the simplest thing to arrange. I have but to send you and a note to the Archbishop of Canterbury at Lambeth Palace, and he will rise from his bed long enough to oblige us both with a special license."

Victor gave a shake of his head, but it was a sign of regret, not denial. Why regret? That the only woman in London who openly disliked him would never agree to marry him? He had no idea; he only knew his head felt as if it were spinning.

"*How* it might come about doesn't matter," Victor said to the queen. "The important part of the equation is the lady's answer. The simple truth is she'd never have me."

Lady Lucianne was on her feet, paler than ever. "What are we talking at here?" she cried out.

"But you would have her if she said she would have you?" the queen insisted.

"You cannot possibly mean me and . . . and Lord Oxenby!" Lady Lucianne said, her hands balled into fists at her sides.

"You think to set a trap," Victor told the queen. "A trap sprung by words." He managed a lopsided smile, for some of his alarm had slipped away in light of the obvious conclusion to this bizarre turn. "But, Your Majesty, your trap holds no bait to entice the prey."

"Ha! I never know if such humility is becoming or vexing. The latter, I think, as it is false. You have much to offer a woman, Oxenby."

"A broken face, for one," he said on a growl, annoyed to hear the bitterness in his own voice.

She waved away his comment. "Does a woman look at the wrapping only, or does she wonder what lies inside the gift?"

"Pretty words, but only words," he countered. He sat up, beginning to tire of the inane, impossible conversation.

"There is much power in a word, Oxenby," the queen told him. "The simple words 'I do,' for instance."

There was now, as always, something undeniably regal in her tones, her every gesture. She'd been queen a long time. He knew she had long since wearied of the role's demands, of the burdens brought to her by the two simple words "I do," and yet, unlike her husband's escape into madness, her role must be played out. There was no escaping it. Such was the unenviable fate of royalty.

She looked spent, yet she struggled on, tonight attempting to find a settlement for her wayward goddaughter. It was noble of her to care, if wrongheaded in choosing him for the role of savior.

"Ask the lady," he repeated.

"But first your word," the queen insisted.

"You have it," he said with a small gesture of his hand, "for all the difference it will make." Victor sat back in his chair once more, feeling his shoulders relax even though his costume's feathers poked at him through the cloth of his coat. This had become nothing more than a game of speculation. The queen might hope to marry off her beloved if troublesome goddaughter, but it would never be to him. Lady Lucianne would rather marry the devil himself than the one man in all England whose company she would reject, given a choice.

"Marriage!" Lady Lucianne cried now. She sat down once more, heavily, as though her legs had failed to support her, her agitation only reaffirming Victor's certainty her rejection would be swift. "Really, Godmama," she said, her voice thin, "you may have called Lord Oxenby my suitor, but he never was. Never would be."

"Never?" the queen threw at her goddaughter. " 'Never' is a very long time, and it is a word spoken too lightly by foolish young people." She pursed her lips and shook her head, then took a deep breath and started anew. "Lucianne, you know what I mean to ask you. I would have you wed Oxenby, tonight. He has said he is willing if you are, and I think he would be glad to end his solitary ways—"

Victor began to protest, but the queen overrode him with a look. He subsided, for any such claims, false or no, changed nothing.

"Lucianne, think of everything a girl must ever be mindful of in deciding to wed. Think of your family, your sister's entrée into society, and think of your own reputation. Think that Oxenby here has said you'd never have him because his face is marred, and to deny him would be to allow him to believe that bit of foolishness."

Both women looked to Victor, and he did not move or turn his head. He silently dared them to stare at the scar that ranged over the right side of his face, that uneven red skin that managed to be ugly and never dashing, as other men's scars sometimes were. Bedamned to them both if they could call it foolishness when he knew how often people's gazes avoided looking at it, avoided meeting his eyes and letting him see the pity in their glances.

"Think of the good you can achieve as a married woman," the queen went on, "and how much more difficult it is for a spinster to achieve those same ends. Do not concern yourself overmuch with the notions of romantic love, for that is a thing for poets, not for real persons."

"Godmama," Lady Lucianne protested weakly.

Her protest went disregarded, for the queen continued. "Romantic love is a fleeting thing anyway, and no guarantee against discontent. It alters with time, for better or for ill, and will not keep clothes on your back and food in your children's stomachs. And that is another thing, Lucianne. Think of children, for you were born to raise them."

Victor allowed one eyebrow to rise in doubt, for he'd long thought Lady Lucianne cool and distant and he'd never imagined her in the role of mother . . . but he'd also been surprised when she'd refused to marry Jerome Holden. He'd considered her before to have no depth, but he knew now that was at least partially wrongheaded. Hers might be a cooler nature, but there was something of warmth in the blood that flowed through her veins, something of discernment.

Perhaps it was time to start anew with her, to forget the past and try to forge a new beginning . . . ? But not tonight, he decided. Tonight must be gotten through, simply enough. He would welcome tomorrow, for it might bring clarity where tonight had only brought vexation and befuddlement.

Lady Lucianne was in no less a thoughtful frame of mind than Victor himself, at least to judge by the serious expression that came over her features. The queen had insisted she think before she answer, had asked her to consider many factors, and she respected that request by folding her hands together and staring at them in her lap, given over to consideration. Victor watched as a half dozen emotions chased across her face, each evaluated, each weighed, as she pondered her decision.

He wondered how much of the woman's thoughts were given over to embarrassment at this ludicrous proposition, but he supposed mostly she was considering how to be kind in her rejection of him.

She'd not been kind before in rejecting him.

She'd been standing with friends at one of the first occasions at which she'd been permitted since making her come-out. She was small, delicate in build, and dressed in palest green muslin, with tiny leaves of ivy wound into the dark hair pinned atop her head. Her brother called her "Elf," and he supposed she'd gone to some trouble to embody the nickname—in any event, her appearance charmed him, as he was getting used to being charmed by this suddenly new and nearly grown-up Lady Lucianne.

He'd been crossing to her side, with no thought more complicated than the desire to stand near her, when an errant draft carried the group's words to his ears.

"I am wearied unto death of wounded men home from the war," one of her friend's complained. "Everywhere you go, you see men missing an arm or a leg . . . Ugh. I wish the war was over."

Everyone agreed, except one young man. "But, ladies! They tell me a scar is the very thing!" he quipped. "I was hoping to join up and get one of my own, in order that I might be seen as dashing."

"Dashing?" Lady Lucianne had replied just as Victor had come to a sudden halt behind her. He meant to retreat, to turn his own scarred face away before he could be drawn into any such discussion, but it was already too late for that. Several pairs of eyes stared at him over Lady Lucianne's heads, even as she went on. "Never say it, Mr. Yarburrow! I for one should be terribly disappointed to see your face marred by an ugly old scar," she said flirtatiously.

Mr. Yarburrow murmured something, eyed Victor where he stood frozen in place, and coughed into his hand.

There was no way for Victor to pretend he hadn't heard. He might have saved the moment with a quip or a shrug, but he'd not been prepared. Her words had lashed out at him, had seemed intended for him specifically, even though he knew they weren't. He'd been thinking only of the pleasure of her company, how she'd altered from his friend's "mere little sister" he'd known for several years. He knew now he'd walked up to her with his usual guard dropped, his defenses lowered.

Even then he'd known she'd not meant to strike him with her words, and so cruelly—but she had.

Belatedly sensing the gazes over her head, Lady Lucianne had slowly turned her head. Color had bloomed in her face at once. "Not all scars are ugly," she had stammered, and he'd watched as she'd realized the words did nothing to assuage the moment. "I never meant . . ." she had tried again.

"I know exactly what you meant," he'd said, his cutting tone as cruel as the blow he'd just taken. "Please excuse me, as I would hate for my appearance to disappoint you terribly, and thereby ruin your evening."

Her head had snapped back as if he'd struck her, but not even the hurt and regret in her eyes had been enough to alleviate his own bruising.

He'd bowed stiffly and retreated, and any dawning adult relationship between them had died at its birthing.

"I will marry Lord Oxenby," Lady Lucianne said, her voice flat but firm.

"What?" Victor and the queen cried together.

For a moment twin spots of darkness filled Victor's vision, but a deep gulp of air chased them away almost as quickly. He was glad for it, because he needed to stare down at her, to confirm by her expression what his ears seemed to have heard.

She looked up at him, at first through her lashes, a stricken look on her face. "I will marry you tonight, Lord Oxenby. For Rebecca's sake," she told him, voice wavering and her gaze pleading. "My sister! She wants to marry. Her dowry—" Words seemed to fail her then—perhaps she saw horrified disbelief in his gaze down at her.

The queen gave a brittle laugh. *"Gott in Himmel!* Lucianne, I just *knew* you would say no, but as always you have surprised me. You go right when I say left, every day of your life—but tonight! Tonight you go left."

She stood also, shaking her head, and for a moment she appeared rattled. It was so rare for the queen to allow herself to look nonplussed that Victor found his alarm doubling.

"And now I have a dilemma." The queen slanted a look between Victor and Lady Lucianne. "I took your vow, Oxenby, but I thought it was all foolishness. What am I to do? Say that I do not hold you to it? When it can do such good? Please to remember that it does good for you as well, for the Oxenby name would be joined to the Gordons of Dorcaster, and no one can label the Dorcaster title as belonging to a 'parvenu.' Your grandpapa would have been proud of how such a connection would move your family name up in the world."

"Your Majesty, I—"

"Words fail you. This is such a surprise. You need a day or two to consider things, I know, I know! But the facts will not change in a day or two. Lucianne will still be in need of a husband, you will have still given your word."

She stopped to consider for a long moment, then closed her eyes and shook her head. "When all is said and done," she said, opening her eyes to skewer Victor with her gaze, "I cannot allow you to insult my goddaughter by breaking your word—which is a favor to you, as well. I must allow you to protect your honor. You will thank me one day."

The clever old witch, Victor thought, eyes narrowing. She was as cunning as any cabinet minister and twice as likely to negotiate for what she wanted in any devious or underhanded manner that suited her purpose. Had she and Lady Lucianne prearranged this?

That would explain much . . . but not the distressed light that lingered in Lady Lucianne's green-gray eyes or the way her hands clung together so tightly that the knuckles had gone white. If she was acting, she was a marvel.

"Our vows would be empty," Victor warned the queen.

"Most vows are fulfilled *after* they are stated, not before," the queen said with a dismissive snort.

"I had not thought of that," Lady Lucianne said quietly, her small, somber voice somehow commanding even the queen's full attention. She glanced up at Victor again. "About any vows. How we'd have to say them." She shook her head. "This is impossible. 'To love and to honor.' We cannot do it. Forget what I said."

There was real agony in her expression, Victor saw just before she covered her face with trembling hands.

There'd been no scheming, except perhaps the scheming that went on in the queen's clever and sometimes ruthless mind. Queen Charlotte had seen an opening and had struck with the precision of a viper—but even Victor had to admit it had all been in an attempt to save this trembling young woman from social ruin or a future of obscurity.

Not just any young woman, but the sister of Victor's friend.

His friend's sister . . . He'd given his word. . . . For a moment, Victor felt as if he could not breathe, could not think. If only he'd stayed in bed today. If only he'd stayed away from the Queen's House. If only he had refused to put his name in the bowl for the masquerade's game . . .

However, "if onlys" were not going to resolve this quandary. He took a deep breath, keeping his arms at his side in order to keep the women from seeing that his hands trembled as well. So then, what alternatives were there? There must be some. What did not harm the lady's status or his own?

They could all pretend it had never happened. No one need ever know of the offer he'd made within these four walls if he did not carry them through—no one but the three of them: his queen, his best friend's sister, and himself.

He could accept Lady Lucianne's withdrawal. He could disappoint the queen in her opinion of his word. He might even be able to convince himself that his promise had been coerced and was therefore invalid.

But he could never look Reuben in the eyes again, not if he broke his word.

"I will tell the archbishop to be furious with *you* for having him driven from his bed," he said to the queen in a tight voice.

"No!" Lady Lucianne said, her voice as pale as the tear-marked face she raised from her hands.

"It is too late to say no, my lady," Victor told her stiffly. "Our queen is correct. There is power in words. And no way to take mine back, even though you desire it." He hesitated, recriminations and excuses and protests all rising to his lips, only to be bit back. None of them would serve. The dice were cast. "I . . . I hope you can forgive me for what must be," he said instead.

Lady Lucianne's throat worked, but no words came forward, no doubt because there was nothing to be said that would change a thing.

The queen shook her head again, even as she moved to her dressing table, on which sat a letter box. "Apologizing for agreeing to marry a woman! Wonders never cease," she muttered as she pulled forth ink and paper.

Victor and Lady Lucianne looked on, awkwardly still and silent, as the queen wrote her missive, applied wax, and impressed the seal with her ring. She then wrote another note, without bothering to seal it.

"I know you will have walked here, so this missive will secure you a coach from my stables," Queen Charlotte said, handing him the unsealed note along with the one with *Archbishop of Canterbury* written across it. "We will be ready for the marriage ceremony by the time you have returned, Oxenby," she added calmly. "There is a vicar in attendance tonight. I will ask him to officiate."

Victor merely nodded, tucked the archbishop's note into his coat pocket, and thought of the distance he must travel, across London Bridge and into Lambeth, and back again. Speed was in order, and the idea of traveling at speed made him scowl deeply.

He turned crisply to stride toward the door. As he pulled it open, he glanced back at the two women, then wished he hadn't.

It *had* to be a sign of bad things to come, to see one's bride-to-be weeping against the royal bosom.

His scowl deepened even more, and he turned back to the door, just as it occurred to him that there would be curious eyes turning his way as he made his way out of the house to the royal mews. He had no wish to surrender the queen's note to the majordomo and then wait for a coach to be brought around. Even though it made a sour taste come to his mouth, he'd go to see to the harnessing for himself. He did not need to enter the stables or place himself too near any ill-tempered horses and their maiming hooves; at least he'd be in one of the queen's well-sprung carriages, he tried to console himself.

It also would have been preferable to go forth unnoted, but think hard as he might Victor could not envision a path to the mews that would not take him past at least a dozen onlookers.

Devil take them all! he cursed to himself as he put up his chin and vowed he'd say nothing, leaving the queen to explain what was about to unfold. He tried to erase the scowl from his face, but all he could manage was closing the door behind him without slamming it.

Chapter 7

Lucy hesitated, horribly conscious that everyone was aware of her hesitation, but she'd never had two more difficult words to utter. Queen Charlotte, not five minutes ago, had scolded her for resisting saying the words at all, telling her to "make the best of things, my girl! That is what every woman must do in this life."

Any further protests had fallen on deaf ears, so Lucy supposed the queen was correct after all, for she found herself about to utter a vow she couldn't possibly mean.

She tried once, her voice coming out as the merest whisper, so that she had to clear her throat. The second time, however, she managed to say shakily but audibly, "I do."

"I now pronounce you man and wife," the vicar said, his words begetting a very unchurchlike chorus of cheers.

But that was hardly to be wondered at, for she was not in a church but in the South Drawing Room of the Queen's House. She, in multicolored troubadour's gown, was marrying a red-waistcoated and feathered Lord Oxenby before a half-drunk crowd of revelers, under the faintly disapproving ministrations of the Vicar Polfield, a masquerader who had been pressed into service despite his pirate's costume.

Not "marrying"—*had* married. The ceremony was over. They'd done this thing.

"You must deliver me to my parish when you leave here tonight in order that we may see to signing the register and giving you your marriage lines," Reverend Polfield told them. If he had further instructions, they were lost to the sudden influx of the masquerade crowd upon the newly married couple.

Lucy gave a squeal of surprise as she was pulled forward and nearly lifted off her feet. "Dance!" someone cried, the chorus being picked up by many others, "The newlyweds must dance!"

As quickly as she'd been pulled toward the center of the room, now she was thrust toward Lord Oxenby. The two of them collided without grace, pressed in on all sides by the noisy crowd, so that Lucy wondered how they could be expected to move, let alone dance. The crowd, giddy with the excitement of the surprise wedding ceremony, however, finally slowly receded.

Only that was worse, for now she and Lord Oxenby were divided out of the sea of people, alone in a circle that had formed around them.

The queen floated toward them, nominally to embrace each of them in turn, but under her breath she muttered, "Smile, children. This is your happy wedding day. We must begin as we mean to go on. Smile!"

Lucy tried to form a smile, but she feared it must look far more like a grimace. Certainly the fixed smile on Lord Oxenby's face was a mere mask, never reaching his eyes.

As soon as the music started, they began to dance. At least it was something deliberate, something that Lucy could pretend to be concentrating all her attention on. She knew she moved woodenly, that her lack of grace was no doubt a trial to Oxenby because of his bad leg, but it was impossible to relax with him so near.

Sweet heaven, she mused, what must he think of all this? Of her? She dared not even look up at him, for fear of seeing the reprehension in his eyes. He must think the very worst of her; of course he did. She did not think much of her own actions, for that matter. Could he understand that she would have thrown her own chances at marriage to the wind, but she'd been unable to be so cavalier with her sister's chances?

If there had been money . . . But Papa had sobbed out that he was broke, finished, sunk. If she'd been unwilling to believe his words, or had tried to explain them away as born of drink, the look on Rueben's face had been more than enough to convince her otherwise. Papa had not merely suddenly become penny-pinching and casual about paying the servants—the money had somehow gone.

With the money gone, so was at least half of the two sisters' dowries. Some of their worth was measured in land—but who knew if the land was lost, too? Had it been wagered away? Must it be sold to keep the family solvent?

Would Rebecca's beau still be willing to wed her without her dowry intact? Lucy did not know Mr. Ellis very well, but what she knew of him she liked. She knew he was truly enamored of Rebecca; he seemed to have eyes for no one else. Lucy also knew, however, that the viscountcy he would one day inherit was one of only "comfortable" income. Any reasonable man might think twice about marrying a woman who brought no land or money to the marriage, and a man of mere "comfortable" income might be expected to do so more than most.

Through marriage Lucy could buy a degree of security for her sister—not just with any monies that Oxenby might be persuaded to provide for a sister-in-law's dowry, but by making Lucy a respectable married woman. Where her reputation had been steadily sliding downward, now it could not be faulted, not from past misdeeds anyway. Marriage wiped the slate clean. While she'd been a millstone around her sister's neck only half an hour before, now Lucy had been transformed into the perfect being for chaperoning Rebecca in her first season. Earl's daughter or no, the unmarried Lady Lucianne Gordon could not advance her sister nearly so well as the married Baroness Oxenby could.

Lady Oxenby.

"Did you catch your hem?" Lord Oxenby asked her with a frown of mild alarm as he prevented her stumble from becoming a fall, his hand sliding around her waist to catch her.

"No," she mumbled. She would never tell him what had caused her to misstep, for it had been realizing that she had a new name. She was Lady Oxenby now. She stepped back, causing his hands to come away from her waist.

Her precedence was greater than his; she could insist on still being called Lady Lucianne if she preferred.

What *did* she prefer? That she not be married to Lord Oxenby, that was what.

That was lightly thought, but it meant dissolving the marriage, never a light thing to accomplish. If by some peculiar miracle they did agree to undo this thing, what would *that* do to her reputation? She shuddered to think of divorce, a thing so rarefied that she had never met a divorced person yet. She knew a divorce was a thing of high financial cost, of awful public humiliation. Claims must be proved against one party or the other, there must be a court trial, an Act of Parliament setting aside the marriage, social ostracism . . . Would Oxenby be willing to undergo such a course? Of course he would not. Such a cure must be judged worse than the disease.

No, there was no undoing what they had done.

Surprisingly, Lucy felt her shoulders relaxing a little. There was no sense in fretting over that which could not be changed . . . especially when there was so much more to fret about.

They were married. She and Lord Oxenby.

Lord Oxenby . . . What *was* his Christian name? she wondered. Merciful heaven, could she have married a man without even knowing his Christian name? But no, no, of course she knew it: *Victor.* Rueben called him by it when he did not call him "Ox" or "Oxenby."

Was it only a few hours ago that she and this man named Victor had danced together for the first time, a dance between near-strangers, near-enemies? And now, fantastically, improbably, dubiously, they were married.

"Please," she said quietly as she heard the music coming to its conclusion, "is there some way we can leave here?"

Lord Oxenby glanced to where the queen stood and grimaced. "Your godmama will not appreciate her Lord and Lady of the Masquerade leaving. However, I think that lady has had all she can expect of us this night."

Lucy nodded and even managed a faint smile. The music ended, and as soon as they'd made their bows to each other, Oxenby put up a hand and turned in a circle. "Your Majesty, my lords, my ladies," he called out. "The newlyweds retire."

There were groans of disappointment, calls to stay, and several people shouted out ribald suggestions for their retirement. Lucy blushed furiously, but Oxenby merely shook his head. "It was our pleasure to lead the masquerade," he announced, "and to surprise you all with our nuptials, but—"

"But you've a surprise of your own waiting, eh?" someone called out.

"Enough!" Oxenby said firmly, but with a smile to mitigate any sting. "Good evening, all!" He took up Lucy's hand, pulling her at once in his wake as he strode purposefully to the queen to make his bows.

Queen Charlotte inclined her head, and Lucy knew with a huge sense of relief that the queen had just permitted them to go. "Good evening, Oxenby," she said, perhaps the smallest of smiles hovering near her mouth. She looked around him to where Lucy quickly remembered to step forward and drop into a parting curtsy. "Good evening, Lady Oxenby," Godmama said, and now she did smile.

"You old cat," Oxenby said, very low. Lucy gasped, horrified that he had said such a thing to Her Majesty, but the queen merely laughed.

"Cats like to pounce," she said. "Even old ones do not sleep *all* the time."

Oxenby bowed again, more deeply this time. "I will remember to watch out for cats who appear to be sleeping, Your Majesty."

The queen, now looking positively smug, looked again at Lucy. "Oh, I have no doubt you will."

Oxenby did not laugh, but the set of his mouth had more of humor to it than it did vexation as they backed away from the queen. He'd never released Lucy's hand, and now he pulled her with him once more, turning and moving through the crowd. He did not stop to talk, merely giving the nod to various acquaintances, and pausing only long enough to collect the Reverend Polfield.

He muttered something as he steered the three of them in the direction of the mews, but Lucy did not quite hear it. Something again to do with "cats" was all she heard, and she thought better than to ask him to elaborate.

His wife stared through the gloom of the coach at the paper in her hands as if she had never seen marriage lines before.

His wife. It had taken less time to be pledged and married than it usually took him to choose the leather he'd like for a new pair of boots.

"They won't fade away if you stare at them hard enough," Victor said of the marriage lines, hoping Lady Lucianne heard the intended humor in his voice. Really, how could they *not* laugh? This situation was too ridiculous for anything else—or at any rate he'd prefer laughter to tears.

"I know," she said without looking up, without smiling.

Her humor was a little lacking at the moment; he could forgive her that. Indeed, he had to grant the lady her due, for she'd not cried, not since he'd left to call upon the severely annoyed and only reluctantly obliging Archbishop of Canterbury. She'd shed not a single tear as she'd said her vows, and if anyone had noted how she had trembled, they had no doubt attributed it to a spot of perfectly normal bridal nerves.

He could not be sure, but he thought perhaps the two of them had managed to seem reasonably happy to be marrying, had played out the illusion well enough that any whispers or questions of impropriety would soon subside. That was some good come of the whole outlandish situation anyway.

Belatedly, he noticed that the carriage was not moving. "Excuse me," he murmured, moving to open the door and pop his head out. He eyed the horses, and tried to ignore that the simple act of noting their nearness made him go cold. "What's holding us up, driver?" he asked the man the queen's stables had provided.

The man, Dinkins he'd called himself, blinked at him over his shoulder, faintly disapproving. "You never gave me a chance to say that I can't take you and the lady to the Warren," he said. "Thought you wanted a private moment or two, so I been waiting to have me say."

Victor shook his head in annoyance at his own lapse, comprehension dawning at once. "Devil take it, I can't go home, can I? Not with a wife!"

"No, sir," Dinkins agreed.

"What is it?" Lady Lucianne—Victor supposed he could now call her simply Lucianne—asked from the coach's interior. A bit of errant light from the lamps on the coach managed to cast her face in shadows.

"My only home in London is a handful of rooms at the Warren," he said, knowing he need not explain that the establishment housed only bachelor gentlemen. Women were not only unwelcome, but disallowed.

"Oh," she said, looking startled. "I . . . I did not think. I suppose I thought we would go to my parents."

Victor nodded at once. "They must be told, of course. And Reuben." He frowned to think of his friend's reaction to their news. He'd been sure Reuben would want him to save his sister from scandal—but now he was not so sure gratitude would be Reuben's sole reaction. He could not imagine how he might react had he a sister and someone suddenly married her without so much as a by-your-leave to her family.

Regardless of Reuben and his family's response, however, Victor had to suppose they would house Lady Lucianne for the night, and presumably himself.

"To Dorcaster House," he told Dinkins, who nodded and turned to set the horses in motion.

Victor quickly pulled the coach door closed and sat back against the squabs. He planted his hands on his knees and let his head hang down to his chest. As always, he sought something else to think about other than that his well-being was at the mercy of one man's ability to control the beasts before the carriage.

Tonight was easier than most when it came to getting lost in other thoughts, not least of which was the likely possibility he would be spending his wedding night alone. Lady Lucianne had already had her share of unwanted surprises tonight; it would be nothing short of ungentlemanly to insist on invading her bed as well.

Ungentlemanly, yes—but that didn't stop him from experiencing a moment of regret. Without lifting his head, he looked out from under his lashes across the dim carriage at the woman he now must call wife, and felt the old pull of attraction he'd always had for her. Any man who had married such a comely woman would have to wonder what she might be like in bed. . . .

This is almost worse than thinking about horses, he thought with a grim interior laugh, then quickly sought a whole other subject to think about.

Another thought did occur to him: He must inform his mother of his marriage. She was all the family he had, not counting some country cousins. He did not know if she would approve of his abruptly gained wife, or the method by which the marriage had come to be, but he was fairly certain she'd be well pleased that he'd finally married at all. She'd refused to let him use the word "bachelor" in front of her, and had frequently made it clear he ought to see about begetting an heir, her grandchild.

Whatever else he might have to endure tonight—make that this morning—Mama was not going to be one of them, he vowed. Tomorrow would be soon enough.

A long silence ensued, broken only when Lady—when Lucianne made a small noise.

"What is it?" he asked through the deep shadows.

"I just remembered I forgot my hat," Lucianne replied. She added tiredly, "Ah, well." She sighed aloud into the darkness, but he did not think it was the hat she was regretting.

She spoke again. "I . . . wish you to know . . ." She stopped and sighed, then plunged on. "I'd never have done it, accepted your . . . offer that way, except for my sister."

"I know," Victor answered her. He'd seen her face, seen the anguish there. He did not know what to make of most of the evening's events, but this one thing he was sure of. She had not accepted his incautious offer for her own well-being, not wholly, not even mostly. She'd done it because what benefited her, benefited her family more.

He doubted she'd change the decision even had she the ability to do it over again, but she had to be regretting it all the same. He was glad for the gloom that largely hid them from each other's sight. He could see the barest outline of her face, could see her lips move, but he could not see her expression, and was glad that she would see little of his either. He was filled with a dozen conflicting feelings, and supposed his expression must be fearsome.

"I'd never have done it either," he added, "except for your brother."

Did her mouth turn up ever so slightly in a soft smile? Impossible to say, just as it was impossible to know what might have caused such a smile. Hearing the truth?

"I have a stupid question for you," she said.

He might have quipped that stupid questions were in keeping with the night's events, but he refrained. "Yes?"

"How do you feel . . . about being married tonight? I mean, of course you are, well, surprised, but . . ." She hesitated, then blurted out, "The thing is, I don't know how to go on! How to act. How to be. Should I pretend for my parents that this is the happiest turn of events, or are we to tell them the unvarnished truth? Or that all this is to be put aside?" He heard the distress in her voice. "Are we to live apart? Or should I act like a wife, or . . . or what?"

He leaned his head back against the squabs for a long moment, then sat upright to look directly across at her shadowed face. "I want to say 'I don't know,' but it won't suffice. So we must decide, here and now. What do *you* want, Lady Lucianne?"

He saw her lift a hand to her forehead, but then it dropped back to her lap. "Surely divorce is impossible?" she asked.

"Agreed. Neither of us wishes that manner of scandal brought down on our heads. And the same is true for annulment, not least because in either course your brother would call me out and no doubt gleefully shoot me dead."

He thought he saw her shudder. "Not to mention

it would undo all the reasons for marrying in the first place. So the marriage goes forward," she summed up. "How? Do I live with my parents? Or in a home of my own? Married, but apart? Or with you? And if so, where?"

He noted her voice did not quaver, although he suspected it was with an effort, for she could not enjoy such questions. He met her courage by summoning some of his own, by searching his soul for honest answers.

"Forgive my long silence," he said when he'd come to his conclusions. "I wanted to be very sure of what I said."

"Yes," she said, very low.

"Here it is then, quickly said as we are nearly to Dorcaster House. If I am to be married, then I will not merely play at it. My wife ought to be at my side, in my home."

Was that a sigh or a bitten-back sob from her? he wondered. At such a moment, it did not signify. What must be, must be. He plunged on. "I have a home in Essex, which we will retire to when the season is over, of course. As for now, we will live with your parents if they'll have me in their house, and we will take a London home of our own as soon as one may be found."

He hesitated, but it was no time to let finer sensibilities stand in the way of understanding. "If I am to be married, I want a family—children, an heir. I want to be loyal to you, and you to me, even if we cannot truly be friends. I want to make the best of things."

He leaned back, as if that might give them both a little more privacy than the close confines of a coach truly allowed for. "I understand that things of an . . . intimate nature may take some time. I want that, too, it is part of life. But not right away, not at once. It must be when you are ready. There's time, time to . . . adjust to each other."

Silence fell, until he felt compelled to speak again, to know what she thought of his demands. "Will this suit?"

"Yes," she said simply, giving no hint of her feelings or thoughts.

He wanted to insist on more, but feared to do so would be thoughtless or bullying. Was it not enough that she had agreed? Why did he need to know how she felt? Would it change anything about their circumstances?

"One thing," she said as the carriage pulled to a halt before Dorcaster House.

Victor hesitated, his hand on the coach door, oddly pleased that she seemingly had a condition of her own to add to his list of how they were to go on. "Yes, Lady Lucianne?"

He was able to see her mouth shape into a fleeting smile. "My one thing is that. My name. Your name. I could call you Lord Oxenby and you could call me Lady Lucianne, but . . ." She paused out of sudden shyness, he thought. "But I propose such formality would add distance between us, which we already have in abundance. Might I be permitted to call you Victor, in private of course?"

"Of course," he said at once. He felt a pressure around his heart, an old familiar feeling he'd had around this woman before, and he had to fight to keep from frowning in reaction to the sensation. "And I shall call you Lucianne."

"Or Lucy, if you like."

He nodded, not speaking, feeling suddenly rather reticent himself. There was intimacy in using a person's Christian name, in being invited into the exclusive club of those who were allowed the privilege. The notion that he had wed struck him anew, and he had no words even if he had felt like speaking.

Instead, he opened the coach door, climbed down, and for the first time ever handed his wife down from a carriage.

He tossed a coin up to the driver, who put his whip to his cap and nodded his appreciation before turning the horses back toward the Queen's House.

Victor faced the front of Dorcaster House and swallowed heavily. Once their news was shared, what would the reaction toward him be within these walls?

It was not Lady Dorcaster who had to sit down upon being told, but Reuben.

"Married?" he echoed, rubbing his forehead with one hand as if he'd suddenly been struck with a headache. "I say! *Married?*"

He, like his parents, was only half dressed. Lord and Lady Dorcaster had been summoned to the parlor from their early morning slumbers, and Reuben had overheard the commotion and come down from his bed on his own. Rebecca, the younger sister, was fortunately still asleep.

"Married at the Queen's House?" Lady Dorcaster asked, staring at her daughter, her hands tightly clasped together. "Well, that was . . . unusual." Her expression lightened. "But how many girls are allowed to marry at the Queen's House? That might be counted as being most singular." She paused, and the doubt returned. "Tell me again, how did this come to be? And who was the vicar?"

Lucianne explained it all again, and Victor let her as he watched Reuben's expression. His friend was clearly shocked.

Even as he thought this, Reuben's gaze shifted to meet his own, their eyes locking. Victor saw doubt and concern there, and he had to fight down an impulse to retreat when Reuben stood to cross to his side.

"Deuce take it, Oxenby!" Reuben blustered by way of greeting. "Could you not have managed . . . I don't know, perhaps a betrothal first?"

Victor shook his head, and slid a glance toward Lord Dorcaster. The man had received the news of their marriage with a loud "Harrumph!" of surprise. When the situation had been explained, he'd scowled heavily, but said, "Well then, what's to be done about it? Nothing, that's what! Marriage is marriage."

Reuben also looked toward his parent, then gave a small groan and an acknowledging nod. "The invested money! It looks bad," he admitted in a low whisper. "I've gone over the books with Papa, and we will have to make considerable economies. Perhaps for years." He glanced at his sister and back at Victor. "I have no idea what will happen around the girls' dowries." He frowned, but it was from vexation rather than incomprehension. "By Jove, I think I am only just beginning to see that you've saved my sister!"

Victor made a protesting noise, even though it was true enough.

"Perhaps the whole family!" Rueben murmured. He had to be considering that one less mouth to feed and clothe was all to the family's financial good, for he scratched his neck and looked away from Victor.

"You'd have done the same," Victor assured him.

Reuben shrugged. "Would depend on how ugly

your sister was," he said, ducking his head, but not in time to hide a quick grin.

Victor took no offense, since he had no sister and since his own brand of ugliness was not the familial kind.

Reuben half laughed and fiddled with the tie to his striped silk housecoat, but then he shook his head and sobered. He looked up, his expression turned serious and thoughtful. "Knew you were the type to take charge and all, but . . . but you've surprised me with all this, Ox."

"No more so than your sister, I'll warrant," Victor said, and despite his friend's serious demeanor, now knew it was all right that he made his own tone light. Reuben was astounded by their news, but apparently had no plan to do Victor violence as a result of it. He would not be calling Victor out—making "an honest woman" of the man's sister was an unlikely cause for a duel—but Victor had braced himself against the possibility of a bloodied nose for form's sake.

Reuben stared at him for a long moment, then slowly smiled again. "Someday you will have to tell me how you convinced her to do it. It can't have been an easy thing."

"It was a necessary thing, anyway."

Reuben shook his head, presumably from amazement, but then his smile widened. "I am overwhelmed . . . but I've just had a wonderful thought about all this."

"Which is?" Victor asked, dubious.

Reuben threw an arm around his shoulders. "You and I, we're now brothers!"

Victor smiled, but underneath a kind of surface pleasure at the thought, he also mentally blew out a breath, suddenly overwhelmed by the thought he'd not only just gained a wife, but a whole new family.

That was not his greatest worry for the moment, however, for Lady Dorcaster had turned to her husband. "It is three in the morning! We must all go to our beds. But . . . but what are we to do with Lord Oxenby?"

All eyes turned to look at Lucianne and then at Victor.

"They are married—" Lord Dorcaster began, sounding as if he were trying to convince himself of the fact.

"And exhausted," Victor said at once, wincing internally at any implication the words had toward physicality. "May I suggest Lady Lucianne go at once to her room, and I share with Reuben?"

Everyone exchanged glances, except Lucianne, who looked to her toes.

"It has been an extraordinarily long day, and I have to think things might be better sorted out later in the morning."

Everyone visibly relaxed, even though Lord Dorcaster gave another "Harrumph!", his scowl somewhere between satisfied and uncertain. Reuben suggested a glass of port, which Lord Dorcaster declined, stating he was going back to bed, and to which Victor nodded. Lucianne was almost immediately gathered up by her mother and hastened up the stairs.

As he waited for Reuben to hand him his glass of port, Victor watched through the open parlor doors as Lucianne mounted the stairs. He wondered what was in her mind. He scarce knew what was in his own.

She stopped halfway up the stairs and glanced back. She blushed when she saw that he watched her, but she offered a nod. Perhaps she meant to say good night, or thanks, or to acknowledge the evening's preposterousness. He could only guess, but he returned a nod of his own.

She turned and continued up the stairs, and Victor turned to receive the glass of port, and hoped that it would prove an aid to sleep.

Chapter 8

Victor rolled his shoulders and stretched his back, and wondered if he might ask for a bedchamber of his own tonight. Reuben's bed had been too soft . . . or perhaps it was having fought the impulse to toss and turn for the remainder of the short night that had left him feeling twinges today.

Certainly sitting while waiting for his mama to come down to her front parlor was not helping. He rose and glanced out the window, then moved to the mantel to finger a china figure there, then paced the length of the room several times before his leg—aggravated from so much activity last night—began to bother him and he sat again.

Lucianne sat still all the while, apparently absorbed by the beading on her reticule. He half scowled her way, then turned his head to stare unseeingly toward a painting above the mantel.

He'd known since opening his eyes this morning that today was going to be filled with problems—not least of which was what to wear. He could have sent for his valet to bring him some things, but he didn't want to wait on the man's having to pack and bring his things. He accepted Reuben's offer of loaned clothing. The coat was a little too long in the sleeve and the breeches a little too large in the waist for him, but preferable to donning the Cock Robin costume once more.

He'd dressed and given a servant a note to deliver to Lucianne, asking her to be ready to call upon his mama in two hours. He would have preferred to see Mama on his own, but he knew she'd have his head if he did not bring her new daughter-in-law—residing not ten streets away from his mama—with him.

He'd then gone home to his rooms at the Warren, striking his valet mute with the news of his nuptials. Worrell had gaped openmouthed, his Adam's apple bobbing as he tried to sputter out his best wishes, but had rallied soon enough under instructions to attend Victor at Dorcaster House.

"Bring everything, I suppose," Victor had instructed him as he pulled a shirt of his own over his head. The rooms he'd taken were furnished, leaving only Victor's personal items to be moved, clothing, brushes, and the like. He could store his belongings in Reuben's room until he'd found a house of his own . . . a house of *their* own, he mentally amended.

Worrell nodded, but he held back the readied cravat from Victor's outstretched hand. "My lord, might I suggest a shave before you venture out once more?" he said, looking instantly relieved when Victor consented.

Now Victor reached up to touch his chin once more, glad he'd freshened up before coming to call on Mama. For that matter, he was glad he'd freshened up before returning to Dorcaster House to take up Lucianne. She'd last seen him in feathered costume, red waistcoat, and yellow stockings—for pity's sake, she'd *married* him dressed thus. What an image to be holding in her head, to add to her regrets.

"Victor!" Mama's voice carried before her, and he could tell by the rising tone of his name, even before he saw her step into the parlor and the note in her hand, that she'd already had the news.

"Victor!" she said again, holding out the missive. "Lady Birmington has sent me a note this morning offering her felicitations upon your marriage! What—" She stopped short, spying Lucianne.

She looked from the wide-eyed Lucianne to her son and back again, and gave a small moan. It quickly rose to a squeal, and she crossed the few steps to take Lucianne's hands in her own and pull her to her feet. "By heaven, it's true!" she said, half laughing. Mama was many things, but slow was not one of them; it had taken her but one glance at Victor's face to know he was not going to deny what Lady Birmington had written.

She released Lucianne, turned to hug Victor to her with another squeal, then turned just as quickly to hug Lucianne again. "But, how? Why?" she asked breathlessly.

"Might we have some tea?" Victor suggested, knowing Mama would not be satisfied with a hasty report, but must have as much of the story as he was willing to give her. The financial state of the Dorcaster household would not be part of the tale, but descriptions of the masquerade certainly must. He'd need some liquid refreshment before she was satisfied, he knew.

Lucianne observed the expressions—surprise, misgiving, mildly horrified amusement—that crossed her new mother-in-law's face as her son explained what had happened. She watched Lady Oxenby—Lucy realized with a start that they now shared the same name. Would Lady Oxenby resent being suddenly thrust into the role of dowager?

She certainly was not the typical representation of a dowager, being a handsome woman with a lively manner and a ready laugh. She was not tall, although still a good four or five inches taller than Lucy, and slender of build. She was dressed in gray today, which somehow managed to flatter the gray in her otherwise dark hair. Her eyes were not as dark as her son's, but they had a spirited spark in them that seemed to make Lord Ox—Victor nervous.

". . . And now here we are, telling you of the marriage," Victor finished the story, reaching for another sip of his now undoubtedly cold tea.

"My!" his mama said. "That was certainly a . . . colorful way to approach matrimony." She put a hand to her bosom. "But, Victor, you must see that it won't do to live at Dorcaster House." Lady Oxenby threw Lucy a quick smile. "Nothing against your family, my dear girl, but it can be . . . awkward to start married life, and more so for the two of you. This was all so unexpected, of course, and you need time to . . . to get to know each other—alone. I mean, you already spent your wedding night apart, which really ought not have occurred. Had you come here I would have arranged a room for the two—"

"Mama!" Victor scolded, lunging from his chair to begin pacing as he had before. Lucy could not miss that the tips of his ears had turned bright red, and she could feel her own doing the same, making her regret she'd removed her bonnet.

"Well, and what is the point of being demure?" his mother returned. "Indeed, tell me your plans. You *are* going to live together, are you not? I do not care that folly has brought you together. We'll have no foolishness about separate households, shall we? Only imagine the scandal *that* would cause, as if the sudden ceremony at the Queen's House, in costume, were not enough!"

Victor stood at the window, his back to the two women, and even from her seat Lucy could see his jaw working. He seemed to be struggling for words, or perhaps civility, so she spoke in his place. "Lady Oxenby—"

"You must call me Anne Marie when we are alone, my dear."

Lucy gave a little bob of her head and a fleeting smile. "I am Lucianne, or Lucy if you prefer."

"Luci-anne and Anne Marie. See, it is destiny!" Victor's mama said on a laugh, looking to her son, who did not turn to join in her mirth. She gave a small, elegant shrug, then gave her attention back to Lucy. "Go on, my dear."

"Lord—that is, Victor and I have not discussed it, my lady, but I think it might be wise if he and I were to remove to the country." The thought had come to her late in the night, just before she'd finally drifted off into exhausted sleep, and had seemed to her as sensible this morning as it had then. They had to start a life together, and that would, without question, be easier in the country than in gossipy, staring, prying London.

She looked up to find that Victor had turned back toward them. He was gazing at her, frowning ever so slightly.

"For a few weeks anyway, I was thinking," she explained to him. "I would not be here for Rebecca, but Reuben would, and we need not be gone the entire season, perhaps. It is just the . . . the marriage was so sudden, and there was the to-do with Mr. Holden"—she saw her mother-in-law's eyebrows rise at that bit of information, which Victor had skirted—"and everything was so . . . ignoble."

The word hit him hard. He visibly winced, and she was reminded of little things Reuben had said, that his friend had been insulted all his life for his grandfather's humble beginnings and for the vivid scar on his own face. "Ignoble" was a word he would not want attached to his name.

Lady Oxenby, on the other hand, seemed undisturbed by the claim. "Pah! Do not go to the country in order to avoid scandal," she advised with a dismissive wave of the hand. "I had my own nine-day's-wonder in my time. It was all anyone spoke of for days: I was to marry Lord Oxenby, bringing him not so little as a penny for a dowry. He married me for my bloodlines. Everyone said I'd 'fallen' and would never dare show my face in society again. But I was glad to marry Oxenby, and for his part he was content to put food on my family's table. He helped my brother finance trade in Indian shawls, which made it possible for Jack to restore the family fortunes. Before he died, my father came to live with us, and Oxenby never said a harsh word to him, even though Papa would lament that he ought to have 'done better' for his girl. As for 'society,'" she said, eyes flashing in memory, "well, Anthony and I, we just went and found some other society to keep!"

She turned a droll look upon her son. "I never minded that I'd 'married beneath myself.' I was happy. Anthony was a good man, very kind to me and wonderful to Victor. He was devastated when the accident happened."

Victor scowled, but he did not turn away again. It was a habit of his that Lucianne had noticed, even from the distance that had existed between them. When others mentioned his scar, Victor seldom looked away, seldom tried to hide it from their gazes. It was raw defiance, of course, and stubbornness, but there was something of courage in it, too.

"I would have been content enough with new friends we made," Lady Oxenby went on, "but it was important to Anthony to make life easier for our children—well, Victor, our one child who lived."

Lost status, lost friends, lost children—Lady Oxenby could have been bitter, but she was not, Lucy thought, beginning to feel humbled. In comparison, what did she have to feel distressed over?

"Anthony had promised his father that he'd build upon the Oxenby name, the same promise Victor gave to Anthony on his deathbed. Both have done what they could to hold to that—"

"Mama, enough," Victor spoke at last. His tone was restrained, his look sober. He flipped back his coat and put his hands on his hips, a gesture that said a decision had been reached. "Lady—Lucianne has the right of it. I think it would be well if she and I retired to Essex for a few weeks, a month perhaps."

Lady Oxenby did not argue. Instead, she stood at once, clasped her hands together, and looked at her daughter-in-law. "May I come with you back to Dorcaster House? I should like to be of assistance in helping you pack if you desire it."

The son was much like the mother, Lucy found herself thinking as she nodded agreement. Both tended to be blunt, decisive, and it would not occur to either of them to pretend they did not understand when they did. They were a candid, brusque people, but there was something also refreshing about their direct manners. They were the sort of people who would not be liked by everyone, but, Lucy suspected, they would be cherished by the ones who did.

She glanced up at her new husband and wondered what it would feel like to be in accord with him, let alone to "cherish" him. The only feeling she was sure of, though, was a tight knot forming in her stomach at the idea of being alone with him. She had not really thought about that side of the "leaving London" equation—but the decision had been made, and she had best get used to the idea of being solely in his company.

Victor paced the front parlor of Dorcaster House, having to step over and around a dozen portmanteaux in order to do so. He could not imagine why they needed so many boxes simply to go to the country for a few weeks, but only a fool would tell a rueful bride that she could not have as many portmanteaux as she wished.

They'd waited one day more, in order to pack and then start out in the morning for his estate northwest of Colchester. It would be one day of driving at a leisurely pace, which Victor far preferred to the breakneck pace of five hours in which a light curricle or phaeton would make the same trip. Still, nice, safe, leisurely pace or no, he'd prefer to get the journey started sooner than later and get it behind him.

"We'll call it a bridal journey, of course," Reuben said, looking not the least bit anxious where he lounged stretched out on a settee, eating toast from a plate he'd balanced on his stomach. "Can't think why you feel the need to leave London at all, but that's how we'll explain it."

Victor didn't bother to answer. Why *were* they leaving London? It had seemed a reasonable suggestion when his mother was insisting on dabbling in matters that were most decidedly not her concern—but in the light of a new day Victor was not so sure avoiding his mama's interference was reason enough to be going. It *did* resemble a retreat . . . but retreating from what? A little gossip? The news of marriage was better than whispers that Lucianne had firmly shelved herself by having yet another public argument with Jerome Holden, surely? He did not think

Lucianne would flee from so little a sting as that . . . so from what did she flee?

The answer was not the gossip, but had to be the man who centered in it—Holden. She did not want to see him, Victor guessed. Did not want to be in the same city as him, did not want to have to enact this new and peculiar married state with him as a witness.

All of which meant that she still cared for the man.

Of course she did. She'd been betrothed to him for two years. She'd be of a low and mean sort not to care for him yet, even though they'd quarreled.

Her caring did not disturb Victor so much as did her choosing to run away. It seemed . . . unlike her. On the other hand, what did he know of Lucianne? They were all but strangers.

"Your scar makes you look absolutely fiendish when you frown so," Reuben remarked. He picked up his plate and dusted toast crumbs from his waistcoat.

"Good to know," Victor said, trying to sound offhand. "If we are beset by footpads, I'll be sure to frown at them."

"Cease your pacing, Ox," Reuben advised, standing and setting his plate aside. "I will go fetch Lucy and tell her it's time to go. She's packed enough to be ready, I say. Go out and get the footmen in after these boxes, eh?"

Victor gave a grateful nod as he stepped out the side door that led into the stable yard and halloed over a pair of footmen. He watched them load the boxes while he eyed the horses already waiting in their traces. Big brutes, strong enough to pull a laden coach, he noted with a scowl.

He didn't look forward to the coach ride, but he would not mind being in Essex once he'd gotten there. He pictured reaching Oxenby Manor, and clicked his tongue at the idea of how distressed his housekeeper would be to have him arrive unexpectedly—not to mention with a new mistress of the household on his arm.

So there was another matter to consider, he thought as he walked back into the house: how his country household would now be run. Victor had no doubt Lucianne would take on the duties designated to her gender. He might not know much about her personality, but he did not believe she would shirk her duties. There would now be regular meals instead of the haphazard dining he'd done at his leisure. There would be parties to give, not simple gatherings of male friends for port and cards. There would be books read aloud and shared of an evening, instead of the solitary silent reading he was used to. There would be chats over dinner. There would be the weekly going to Sunday services, he presumed, which was largely his habit anyway. There would be the fuss of Yuletide logs brought in, of birthday gifts exchanged, of local weddings, layings in, christenings . . .

He felt his heart lurch, momentarily stunned by the idea that he might one day be a father. Before today, he'd given up the expectation, determined to remain alone so that his marred face would offend no female sensibilities. He'd grown used to the idea that the eldest son of one of his far-flung cousins was to inherit when he was gone. This new thought, this new possibility, unnerved him.

"Here she is, ready at last." Reuben's voice intruded on Victor's thoughts.

He lifted his head, his gaze falling at once on Lucianne, dressed in a carriage dress of pale blue with a matching jaconet-covered bonnet. It flashed through his mind that he would have to be sure she ordered some new gowns now that she was married and could wear a greater number of hues. Dark blue would have been more appropriate for the dust and dirt of travel, but the boldness of dark blue was allowable only as an accent color for unmarried ladies, so she had no such palette in her wardrobe from which to choose.

All the same, she looked very fetching in the gown he'd never seen on her before. There was so much he did not know of her, forgetting such witless things as the nature of her ensembles. What did she like? Did she dance because she loved to, or because it's what one does? Did she prefer coffee over tea, or the other way around? Was she a bruising rider who would never understand his fear of horses should he be so stalwart as to tell her of it? Was she an observant sort who would note his apprehension even though he did his best to hide it from others? Did she like to dig in the garden? Did flowers make her sneeze?

He shook his head. How could he ponder the idea of future children when he could only guess at how this woman would feel in his arms? For that matter, would she ever wish to come into his arms? He'd claimed that intimacy must be part of their bargain, but a claim did not a reality make.

He wondered briefly if he'd be willing to take her to bed if she was willing to "do her duty" yet remained aloof or cool toward him . . . but then he could only laugh at himself, knowing that a physical willingness on his part would never be the problem. He'd never had a kept mistress even if he'd had his share of tumblings with willing barmaids and their ilk, but a life of chastity had never been part of his plan for remaining a bachelor. It would be ironic if it became his misfortune now that he was married—ironic, but never by his choice.

But there was time, plenty of time. Before he bedded his wife, he thought it might be wise to try to woo her.

There was yet another staggering thought: It behooved him to woo this woman, this stranger. He owed her a courtship. Could he do it, court Lucianne? Did he want to? Did it matter whether or not he wanted to? Could he put aside old prejudices? Could she? He tried to think of kissing her, of her hands coming up to his face, fingers tracing his scar . . . and the vision faded, as ruined as was his face.

"Victor? You've gone all pale," Reuben said near his ear, a hand under his arm as though to keep Victor from sliding to the ground.

"Sorry," he mumbled, straightening his stance and mentally shaking himself. "I was woolgathering. Lady Lucianne, you are ready?"

She gave him a look—perhaps a brief censure for having forgotten and attached "Lady" to her name—but she nodded. She also looked pale, but he was fairly certain she had not been crying.

"I've already said farewell to Mama and Papa," she said, reaching up on tiptoe to slip her arms around Reuben's neck.

"Did you say good-bye to Rebecca?" Reuben asked.

It was as if the question summoned the young woman, for she appeared on the stairs, moving rapidly down them. She was as pretty as her sister, with hair just as dark, and a fringe over her forehead where Lucianne had none. The girl was closer to Rueben's height than Lucianne's, and her face was more given to traditional beauty, more rounded and therefore less elfin. Victor thought with a fleeting humor that their three dark heads were stair-stepped when they stood together. She was newly from the schoolroom, so that Victor had little knowledge of her beyond the occasional affectionately exasperated comment from the six-years-older Reuben.

Tears were teetering on Lady Rebecca's lashes, but she tried for a brave smile. "You'll be back soon?" she asked her sister in a shaky voice.

"Soon, my love," Lucianne assured her as they slid into each other's arms.

Lady Rebecca turned to Victor, offering him a curtsy, to which he bowed. "I wish that I might have more time to make your acquaintance, Lord Oxenby, but that will happen when you return to London, I do hope," she said politely. He had "stolen" her sister unexpectedly from her side during the girl's first season—he might have expected resentment, but all he sensed now was a bit of chagrin perhaps.

"That is my hope as well," he said.

Duty done, the girl turned back to Lucianne and threw her arms around her once more.

Victor put out his hand to Reuben, who clasped it and used it to pull his friend into an embrace. "Don't stay away too long, Ox," he warned with a waggle of his eyebrows as he stepped back, "or else I'll grow so bored that I'll go out and also find myself a wife."

"Make sure she's not ugly," Victor said, recalling the previous night's conversation.

Reuben laughed, but Rebecca had begun to cry. "Oh, go!" she said, pushing herself away from her sister's embrace with tears freshening in her eyes. "Go before I blubber and make a fool of myself."

"Too late," Lucianne said, tears also flowing as she drew her handkerchief from her reticule and handed it to Rebecca. The younger girl gave a burbling half laugh, half sob, took the handkerchief, then turned and dashed away up the stairs.

"Come," Victor said, taking Lucianne's elbow to lead her forward, for he was fairly sure she was half blinded by tears.

Once she was seated in the coach, she accepted his handkerchief in replacement of the one she'd given Rebecca, weeping silently into it for several long minutes. It was not until she'd controlled her tears enough to give him a bashful smile as thanks that Victor realized he'd forgotten to note the lurch of the coach as they'd begun their journey. That first lurch was always one to make his stomach flip over, a sensation he both expected and deplored—and yet today he'd not experienced it. He'd been distracted by Lucianne's distress, too aware of how he'd changed her life to pay attention to what was commonplace.

He closed his eyes and breathed slowly, trying to tamp down any dread that came with realization. He would do well enough as long as they were on London roads, with his usual driver at the box, a steady fellow who knew better than to drive daringly in the heavy city traffic. But once they were on the rough country roads . . .

Victor knew his thoughts made no sense, for the crowded conditions of London lent themselves far better to the possibility of accident, of collision and mayhem . . . but there was something about the open roads of a country lane that urged speed and a lack of mindfulness in coach drivers. Not to mention the horses, especially as they neared a place that smelled of home. They grew excited and resisted being held back. They wanted to be given their heads, to run full out. They gave themselves over to speed, incapable of knowing that with speed, with flying hooves, came danger . . .

He opened his eyes, aware of his hands clenched atop his thighs, and found Lucianne giving him a quizzical look. He could not pretend to be utterly calm, so he allowed himself a deep, shaky breath, and slowly let it out again. He opened his hands into a relaxed mode even though his primary instinct was to reach instead for the carriage strap near his head. "I hate good-byes," he said by way of explanation.

"Me, too," she said, accepting his rationale.

They fell into silence, he so as to avoid speaking when he was not sure of the steadiness of his voice, and heaven knew what thoughts she kept to herself.

Victor looked out the window, not minding the passing of scenery. It was not the movement that bedeviled him, but the knowledge of the muscled energy that made movement possible. He could, in fact, often distract himself from thoughts of the great beasts harnessed before the coach by gazing at the sights beyond the carriage. At the moment, however, all he could think was that their "bridal journey" had begun with her tears and his dread—hardly an auspicious beginning.

Chapter 9

"Tell me why the little village nearby is called Oxenbury and not Oxenby," Lucianne said.

Victor looked away from the monstrous painting of his grandfather—a piece well executed, if horribly outsized for the room in which it hung from ceiling to floor—and gave a lopsided smile. "Ah! Thereby hangs a tale."

He motioned for her to sit in one of the chairs placed near the book room's grate. Its welcome blaze added warmth to the March night, and she was glad to sit before it now that she had been given a tour of the room. She'd glanced at the book room earlier when the housekeeper, Mrs. Raleigh, had shown her the entire house, but it had only been a quick look.

Now she noted some finer details, beyond the eye-stretching portrait of the first Lord Oxenby. The room's molding and the frieze were finely carved, albeit not grandly ancient; Victor had told her the house was only fifteen years old. The carpets were new enough to still have vibrant greens and yellows, and the curtains were dark green damask over near-sheer ivory muslin undercurtains that would let in the light during the day.

They had retired from the evening meal to the book room, which Lucy supposed they often would as it was of a size to be easily warmed with a fire, and they could read or write letters. If she sat between two of the lamps now lit, she'd even have enough light by which to stitch. It seemed so odd, to be evaluating Lord Oxenby's home, to be imagining herself here day after day.

He sat opposite her, absently watching the flames leap on the grate. "Oxenbury as a village came to be after my grandfather chose to build his home here," he explained.

"Oh. So the village took its name from his title, not the other way around."

"Just so." He looked at her then, something cautious in his gaze. "You must already know that my grandfather was the first to have the title bestowed on him. He developed a better method for forming shot for rifled arms, and made a fortune from it. Our king granted him a barony for it as well, which came with this land upon which we now reside."

He gave a small bob of his head, the gesture of a man remembering. "My grandfather was a crusty old bird. He knew he was full of bluster, and common as the day was long. He was also one of the strongest men you ever would have met, not tall but solid and broad-shouldered. When told that he was to have a title, he knew he'd never be accepted by polite society."

Here Victor's mouth turned up in a soft, fond smile. "But instead of his title sitting poorly on his shoulders, he embraced it with . . . vigor might be the word. When the king asked him by which title he wished to be known, Grandpapa said, 'Ox,' which had long been his nickname. They quibbled, the story goes, because the king refused to title 'any man of mine after a brute animal,' so that eventually it was agreed my grandfather would be called Oxenby."

He looked around the room. "This house was built,

with Grandpapa living in it not quite one month before he died. The village sprang up for the convenience of the builders and then the crofters who work the land for us, of course. Grandpapa thought 'Oxenby' to be a great jest he'd shared with the king, and he thought it unfitting that the village should be named after a jest, so he managed to get the name changed a bit in the royal register. Made it sound 'more proper-like,' he said. He always wanted things to be good and proper for us."

He fell into silence, gazing once more at the flickering flames, and Lucy considered the word "us." "Us" meant Victor; his mama; the household staff; the staff who worked the gardens and the stables; the people who worked in the handful of shops in the village; and the crofters who farmed the land in exchange for a share of the harvest and a roof over their heads.

Lucy was a piece of all this now, a part of "us." It did not matter that she had not expected this part to play. It did not matter that she had been Lady Oxenby only for two days—the duty was now hers.

It struck her that by marrying, she had been transformed. She was no longer Lady Lucianne Gordon, a young woman with few obligations. She was mistress of this fine house, a person of importance—not so much for the title Victor's grandfather had earned, but for the duties that now fell to her. She'd had no time to consider *this* side of marriage, and the realization staggered her, even though she'd been trained her entire life to play this role.

"I will have to meet the tenants," she said aloud, hearing the uneasiness in her own voice as Victor nodded agreement. Then, too, she must set a schedule for the servants to follow, must meet daily with Mrs. Raleigh to plan the day's events and menus.

She must meet the locals, learn of needs that were not being addressed, must go to church in a new place, meet the vicar, the ladies' societies . . .

Upon their arrival in late afternoon, she'd changed out of her traveling clothes in a room hastily denuded of its Holland cloths. Then she'd been given a tour of the house by Mrs. Raleigh, a white-haired and capable lady who had by then sufficiently recovered from the shock of having an unexpected new mistress thrust upon her. Everything had been well enough in order, Lucy had been glad to see, if one discounted the naturally unreadied room and unplanned meal that had to suddenly be prepared.

Lucy had requested a tray of tea and biscuits in her room, which was now dusted, aired, and with a cheery fire on the grate. It was a pretty set of chambers, done in rose and cream colors, and she suspected it had been used by the prior Lady Oxenby when she was there. It felt odd to think she had displaced her new mother-in-law, although there were a half dozen other rooms that would suit when that lady came to Oxenby Manor. Replete with tea, Lucy had then wandered about the gardens, mindful that her new husband was tending to business matters with his steward, but she saw no sign of them.

She'd gone back to her room—it had a door that adjoined it to the room she knew was Victor's—and unpacked with the help of the servant who had been designated as her lady's maid. When there was nothing of her own left to unpack, she'd gone to help his mildly disapproving valet unpack Victor's things. it hadn't been long, though, before she'd opened one portmanteau to find a collection of Victor's smallclothes—at which time she had fled the room.

She'd found the back parlor, which had large windows that gave plenty of light, and read one of her favorite books that she'd brought with her. When her eyes had started to close and her head to nod, she'd gone back to her room to nap for several hours. She'd been woken by the maid, Ginny, in time to dress for supper.

Looking back on how she'd spent her day, Lucy saw that she'd not been acting out her part as she ought. No doubt the housekeeper had been befuddled as to what to serve for supper, having received no instructions from the new mistress. Lucy sat in her husband's book room and realized she ought not have indulged in any misgivings or regrets upon marrying the one man she'd never envisioned marrying; she should have completed her charge regardless. She felt shame heat her cheeks that it had taken her hours to comprehend this simple truth.

"Is it too warm in here?" Victor asked her, no doubt seeing the color in her face. "I could open a window."

"No, no, I am well," she assured him, even as her gaze assessed him. He'd been in a peculiar, pensive mood all day, and remained so now. In the coach he'd been a bit overly talkative, giving her a running description of the fields and towns as they passed. He'd only grown quiet when the coach went over a length of uneven road, and he'd positively blanched when they'd heard the driver yelling to his team.

She had remembered a girl she'd known in childhood who absolutely could not sit in any backward-facing seat in a carriage or else she'd end by heaving up her dinner. Lucy had wondered if Victor suffered from the same affliction—but he'd declined her offer to exchange seats with him.

He had something of the same perturbed look about him yet tonight—but she probably did as well. It was impossible to ignore that they were alone now.

Even the servants had retreated to the recesses of the house, not to be summoned back until the lord or lady of the manor tugged upon a bellpull.

"Victor," Lucy said, gathering all of her wits and courage by staring down at the toes of her shoes that were showing just at the hem of her skirts.

"Hmmm?" he said, shifting in his chair.

"It is our third night together. And now we are here . . ." She could have expanded that, could have said "alone together," but he had to be aware of it as keenly as she was. "I . . . I don't know what you expect of me. As a wife." She shook her head, feeling her blush deepen. "I don't mean household duties or the like, I mean . . ." Words failed her.

"I know what you mean," he said quietly. "Your question has to be 'How soon?' How soon are we to . . ."—he fished for a word—". . . be carnal with each other."

She could not look up at him, but she could nod. "Yes."

"Tonight is the logical answer, because the servants will note . . . any remoteness in our sleeping arrangements. But devil take the servants!" he said, sitting forward in his chair, his motion jarring her vision up to meet his.

The movement was not enough apparently, or the weight of her stare was too much perhaps, because he lunged to his feet, taking an agitated but earnest stance, and half turned toward her. "Let them whisper what they will. I'll not choose my course to suit servants' or family's or anyone else's expectations! I don't love you, and you don't love me, and we are not animals to rut in any season but that of our own choosing."

The words were raw and unpretty, and for a moment they seemed to rob him of speech, but a shake of his head and a scowl were enough to let him go on. "Let us make it perfectly clear between us then! Madam, I will not approach yourself, your bed, your . . . favors until you ask me to do so."

His words faded away as they stared at each other, and she wondered if he truly understood what barrier he had just raised between them. If *she* could see it, almost a physical thing there between them, then surely he could?

The decision was to be hers alone? She would have to *ask* for him? She would have to guess what was in his head and hope that it aligned with her own choice?

Would she ever have that kind of courage?

She was the first to drag her gaze away, for she realized what a wondrous and terrible gift he'd given her. *A bridal gift,* she thought with a grim, dark humor.

He seemed about to say more, but then he pressed his lips together. He blew out a breath, then turned to make her a rather formal bow. "Good night then," he said.

"Good night."

Lucy watched him go out into the hall, shutting the door behind him. She followed in his wake, moving up the stairs to her bedchamber. When she'd closed the door behind her, her gaze drifted to the dividing door that separated her room from his. She stood still a long moment, frowning, but then she crossed to it, turning the key resting in the lock with a soft click. She closed her eyes against a sudden, strange pain in her middle, a pain that ought logically to be in her brain with its madly tumbling thoughts, but which oddly seemed centered very near her heart.

Whatever the future held, she did not think it

would be manifested tonight, not now that she had secured this door. She very much doubted he'd use the one to the hall—no, not uninvited, he wouldn't. She not only took him at his word in this matter, but for a moment resented what he'd done. He'd shifted all the decision onto her . . . but neither did she unlock the door, instead taking the key from the lock and laying it on her mantelpiece.

Chapter 10

Victor looked across the field soon to be planted and saw his wife riding at its far edge. She was far away, but he guessed it was her both from the look of the horse and that its rider was on a sidesaddle. Yes, that was definitely Lucianne's curly beaver hat, styled a bit lower in the crown than a gentleman's was, and her brown riding habit. It was the darkest gown she'd owned as an unmarried woman, the color chosen in defense against the inevitable dustiness of riding. Her new habit, ordered just yesterday along with a dozen other new gowns, would not be ready for a fortnight.

Besides the new gowns, there were other things coming into his home to remind him that he was married. There were fresh greens artfully arranged in the front parlor almost daily, and once there had been a posy of spring hyacinths. It was the kind of feminine touch that Mrs. Raleigh thought important for special occasions but would not bother with otherwise, whereas Lucianne liked something of nature's beauty in the house every day. There was now always a small pitcher of cream on the tea table because Lucianne often liked some in her tea. It had felt both strange and like old days to have another person in the family box at church of a Sunday. A few invitations to Lord and Lady Oxenby had arrived in the post, despite the fact that he and Lucianne had yet to call upon their neighbors.

What he noticed most, though, was the almost daily addition of music to the household. In the past he'd played the violin when the urge came upon him, and Mama would play the pianoforte occasionally when she was in residence, but Lucianne played frequently. She would either play the piccolo or the pianoforte, the latter of which she had not quite mastered. He rather liked coming into the house to music, not even minding the times Lucianne played something over again, trying to get it right. There was something . . . "comfortable," that might be the word, about the sound of someone trying, learning, practicing.

They might be wed in name only, Victor thought now as he watched his wife ride, but he was beginning to feel "married," for there was more to the estate of marriage than merely a nuptial bed. A marriage was a partnership, a joining of resources, and it was companionship. This last thought made him frown for a brief moment, for it was the one thing he wondered most about: how the two of them might physically form a family but never have a meeting of the minds, never that easiness that marked a true partnership.

He'd told himself that he must woo his wife, but it was a more complex thing than he'd imagined. In a fit of chivalrous idiocy he had said she must ask him to her bed—he'd vowed to woo her, then made it so that any attempt to do so would seem an encroachment on his promise to her. Truth was, he'd come running if she so much as crooked her finger at him.

"No doubt about it, Oxenby, you're a fool," he told himself on a sigh.

Even at this distance, he could see she was enjoying herself. He wished he could join her, but it was impossible. He'd tried, many times, to ride over the years, but the panic was too great. He could not fight it off. He'd rather face ten of Bonaparte's infantrymen than try to mount one timid pony. Some men had rational fears, such as spiders or snakes, but the unnatural fear of horses was Victor's curse.

"Not to mention my face," he said aloud, since no one was nearby to hear it. In the two weeks they'd been married, Victor had occasionally caught Lucianne looking at his scar. He'd recently tried his usual trick of staring back at her boldly, but she had not looked away as he'd thought she would.

"Does it hurt?" she'd asked one day.

He'd shaken his head, walked away, and avoided her company until supper.

Now she caught sight of him, lifting her arm in a greeting salute. He wished she'd always hold onto the reins with both hands, even though he'd seen for himself that she was quite capable as a rider. If the world had been made to suit him, no one would ride horses, but it was not. He'd never tell her to cease riding, and intellectually he understood that she was largely safe enough— but that did not mean he had to enjoy watching it.

She spurred her horse toward him, the simple act of her coming his way making a small smile replace the frown of misgiving he'd been sporting. "Isn't that a change?" he said to himself as he watched her ride closer.

Two weeks ago he never could have imagined a feeling of pleasure at the idea of Lady Lucianne approaching him. A stirring of desire, ruthlessly quashed, perhaps, but not pleasure. The explanation was hardly surprising: In living in proximity, he'd learned there was a sweet side to Lucianne.

It was not so much that she'd been unusually kind or solicitous of him. Indeed, at times the tension between them was as taut as a clothesline, especially of an evening. During the day it was: "Did Mrs. Raleigh find the spare key to the tea chest?" and "We've decided to put hay in that field and rye in the northern-most"—the everyday prattle of everyday life. The days were easy, because they were easily filled with chatter and tasks.

However, the nights after supper seemed long. The two of them tried to sit and talk a bit or read aloud to each other or play at cards or musical instruments. The nights boiled down to just them, bound together but not connected, geographically close but physically distant. The shadows reminded them of what they were and were not to each other, and the reminding was awkward.

Just as he was seeing little glimpses of her softer side now and then, her smile now greeted him across the distance remaining between them. "Someone has grown Dutch tulips over there!" she called when she was near enough to be heard, glancing back over her shoulder to indicate the direction from which she'd come. "Spring has arrived, I think."

Victor tried to smile back, but he realized too late that she meant to ride abreast of him before dismounting. He glanced about, desirous of a fence or a post or a tree to put between himself and the horse, but there was nothing. He backed up anyway and swallowed hard.

As he'd thought, she pulled the horse to a halt before him, not six feet away. Victor retreated farther, feeling how wide his eyes were even while he stared hard, his pulse pounding in his neck. Lucy shifted, effortlessly releasing herself from the pommels of her sidesaddle, then looked to him with outstretched arms. "Would you help me down?"

The horse, unrestrained by rein or hand, shook its head and snorted, and Victor saw spots before his eyes. "Just a moment," he managed to mutter, breathing deeply even as he backed up farther still, half-blind and on shaking legs.

The spots cleared in a moment, but he could not seem to make his legs step forward. He closed his eyes, shook his head, and stepped forward woodenly out of sheer force of will, only belatedly opening his eyes. He stood near the horse's side, knowing he could spring away before the creature could realign itself to kick him, but staring wildly at its legs all the same. He kept his eyes fixed even as he reached up, the stiffness of his arms at odds with the trembling in the rest of his body. When her hands had slid down the length of his arms and she was safely on the ground, he immediately retreated.

"Victor?" Lucianne asked, looking puzzled. She had to be noting his skin gone pale and clammy, and his rapid, shallow breathing. He took several steps farther away from the horse and consequently from Lucianne.

It was as if a cloud crossed over her face, wiping away her smile, bringing consternation into her eyes.

"I'll not ask for your assistance again, I assure you," she said coldly.

She thought he had disliked, even *loathed* her touch. He saw it in her hurt expression, in the angry set of her shoulders as she turned away from him. She strode away, leaving him alone with the horse, leaving with entirely the wrong impression.

He opened his mouth to call after her, but what would he say? *Forgive me, I'm the biggest infant in the world, terrified of big, bad horses?* That, rather than hating her touch, he'd been trembling at the nearness of an equine? His desire to soothe her feelings was directly at war with his desire to maintain a semblance of control, of rationality.

Then it was too late anyway, for she'd walked too far for him to do anything but shout after her, and he was not going to shout out this bit of information for all the county to hear and thereby make an even bigger fool of himself.

Neither was he going to bring the horse along by the reins, no matter that it was the most expensive horse in his stables. His groom, Quentin, would fetch it home, or else it would come on its own when it grew hungry for oats.

Victor turned to retreat to the house, choosing a path perpendicular to the horse so that he could keep one eye on it as he moved away. The farther he moved from the animal, the more calm was restored to him, his gait loosening and his breathing returning to normal.

"When I get to the manor, I'll explain to Lucianne," he told himself, doubting even as he thought it that he really would. How could he ever explain it? She'd think him half-mad, as indeed the few others who knew of his affliction did.

He went to the house, but he did not seek Lucianne. In a brooding mood, he instead made his way down the stairs to the basement, where the kitchens were.

"M'lord," his Irish cook greeted him, evidencing no surprise to see him there. Cook reached for a bowl covered with a linen cloth and handed it to his master. "Yer arrived just in time," he commented in his Dublin accent.

Victor shrugged out of his coat and waistcoat, and

secured one of the kitchen aprons around his middle. He lifted the linen from the bowl, aware that his hands had ceased to shake. Beneath the towel was a yeast dough, now risen to a nice, rounded height.

"Perfect," Victor said. "I am in the mood for punching." He slammed his fist down into the dough, and smiled grimly.

Lucy sat in the shadows of the kitchen stairs. She'd been there nearly half an hour, watching Victor pound a risen dough down into a ball, which he had then flattened into a rough rectangle with a dowel. He rolled this up from one end to the other, forming a spiraled log, then tucked it seam side down in a bread loaf pan, and buttered the top.

It was not so much that he obviously did not mind getting unkempt and flour-dusted that amazed her, but that he displayed an expertise that spoke of long habit. He'd made bread many times before.

She noted with interest when he began a new batch, adding in the yeast and eggs and sugar and all, but also that he stirred in anise and currants. She thought of the night they'd married, the night they'd eaten buns spiced with anise and currants, and determined that Lord Oxenby had remembered, too.

Who would have guessed at this little pastime of his? Not she—just as she would not have guessed that her touch, however casual, would be repugnant to him. At night, when they sat together and played cards or read, she'd thought . . . well, she'd thought there had been an awkwardness between them, a tension hardly to be wondered at—but not a return to the old animosity, surely?

She sighed to herself, shook her head again in confusion, and turned up the stairs without making her presence known.

So, her husband liked to work with bread, she thought as she wandered slowly toward her chambers. She gave a small laugh, not of derision, but continued surprise.

It was a rather common thing to do, she supposed, revealing the shallowness of the Oxenby roots—but it was strangely appealing, too. Her father might go shooting in order to expend vexation; Reuben would probably go carousing. Other men hunted after foxes, or played at fisticuffs at Gentleman Jackson's saloon, or attended cockfights.

Victor baked bread.

A smile touched Lucy's mouth, but it was as fleeting as the moments of peace between them. This marriage, little more than a fortnight old, remained a strained and inept thing. She had taken on the mistress's duties, a painless thing as Mrs. Raleigh had run the household well and Lucy had simply nodded to much of what the woman already had in place. Victor had spent time over the estate books, walking the land, meeting with his steward—taking on the master's duties. They had a marriage, a functioning union, and yet it was not whole, not complete—not real.

She'd thought more than once of asking Victor to her bed, just to get the moment behind them, thinking it might ease them into a more genuine married state. But it was one thing to think it would serve, and so much easier than acting upon that thought.

What was there to wait for, though? she mused. Love? He'd said it plainly enough: They did not love each other. She'd not been able to protest the bald statement even if it had seemed harsh and unhopeful. What then? A companionable nature between them? What was that? Would she know it if it unfolded between them? Did they wait upon some secret sign, some magic moment?

"Perhaps senility?" she muttered to herself, once again smiling a little even if it was at her own sour quip.

She gained her room, and changed her gown with the help of her maid. As Ginny brushed out her hair, preparing to put it back up for the evening meal, Lucy stared at the door that remained locked between her room and Victor's. She shook her head, making Ginny "tsk!" at her, and turned her thoughts to what she'd discovered about her husband's estate.

She'd been raised to know what was expected of the mistress of a grand house, one facet of which was making the rounds among the tenants and seeing how the hardships of their lives might be relieved. There were Boxing Day gifts, of course, the day after Christmas, and foodstuffs were handed out during lean times, and gleaning after the harvest was brought in was encouraged. But it was more than that. It was also seeing that roofs were mended, and new wells dug, and cloaks provided for those who had none in winter. It was knowing one's tenants well enough to be sure they did not suffer.

She'd made such rounds with her own mama and knew what to look for. She saw some things on Victor's estate, those things a woman was more likely to note than a man: that the increasing Mrs. Sullivan did not yet possess a cradle for her first infant; that the Beeson family had a shortage of blankets; that the pensioned old butler's infected foot was not healing properly and required a surgeon's tending. But mostly she saw clean if small homes, with sturdy roofs and beds enough for the occupants within, and that the crofters who worked Victor's land did not have the hollow-eyed look of overwork or starvation about them.

Victor had hired a good steward, clearly.

Still, it had to be conceded that the steward could only be as good or generous as his employer allowed him to be—which meant that Victor was a good and generous lord to these people.

Not that she'd ever imagined Victor being actively cruel, but if she had given any thought to the matter before, she would have guessed he'd be cold and remote toward them, as he'd been to her. But the residents of Oxenbury greeted him with respectful nods and calls of "good day to you, my lord," or its like. They did not dislike or distrust this man. A crofter's life was hard, make no mistake, but for Victor's tenants at least it was not grim.

Dressed for supper, she came down to the dining room to find the object of her thoughts waiting for her. Victor stood reading a book, which he tilted to best advantage next to a lit candelabra. While he might be the grandson of a parvenu, his manners were those of a gentleman, for he would not seat himself at table until he'd first seen her seated, not even merely to read.

He turned when she entered, putting aside his book. "My lady," he said, as he did most evenings, moving to pull out her chair.

She sat, and then could not repress a smile, for before her sat a wicker bowl filled with buns. They were fragrant with the scent of anise and dotted with currants.

Servants moved quietly to serve them as Victor began to tell her the details of his day. "We've a fence down on the south boundary, ten feet of it or so. Howell thinks some lads were steeplechasing. Poorly, I might add. But he wants to get it fixed before we put in the corn, to keep our neighbors' cattle out, of course."

The servants moved away from the table, leaving Victor free to reach for his goblet of wine, from which he took a sip. He considered Lucy over its rim for a long moment, then set it back on the table. "There's a thought—our neighbors. You have met most of them at church, but since we are here only a couple weeks or so more, we ought to consider hosting a party so that you might meet everyone who is not presently in London."

"I hadn't considered a party," Lucy said. It only made sense though, since Oxenby Hall normally was to be her home five or six months of the year, the place where they would retire when the season was ended.

"We do not have to if you do not—"

"No, no," she assured him, thinking he looked disappointed. "It is a fine idea. We can make up a list of whom to invite after supper."

"Very well," he said, and she could see she had pleased him. She looked to her plate, finding it strangely difficult to hold his gaze when he looked at her with this gently approving smile that she'd never before known he possessed.

For that matter, when he did anything that was kind or charming it only made it more difficult for her to imagine asking him to her bed. Gentlemanly behavior softened his rough edges and lessened old stings, but it also made him into something he had not seemed before.

He was not her friend, but she could no longer think of him as the enemy. He was her husband, but not her lover. They lived intimately, but they were not intimate.

There were moments when something he said or

some expression he offered moved her. She might laugh at a jest he'd made, or flush with pleasure at his praise for some task she'd seen completed. She could at last understand why her brother had taken this man as a friend, a crony, a confidant . . . and the understanding made the thought of lying with him only more difficult to imagine acting upon. Even though they could not pretend at having two hearts entangled, still the man had engaged something in Lucy's mind. They'd made a connection of some sort, ill-fitting them both and yet undeniable.

Whatever else that connection was, it was also a cackling little demon that sat between them as they dined or when they played the violin and piccolo of an evening. It was the whisper that mingled with Victor's voice when he took his turn reading aloud. It was the impish shadow that followed her up the stairs and made her turn her head for one last glance back at the man from whom she'd just hurried away.

The odd, frustrating, sense-tingling demon of a connection was there again tonight, now that they had left the supper table and moved as usual to the book room. To Lucy it felt as if it filled the book room, an invisible fog that crept into her nose, her lungs, her belly. Victor, though, seemed untouched by it, nonchalant where he sat opposite her, one leg crossed over the other and gently swinging to and fro.

Lucy fought to concentrate on the guest list she and Victor were compiling, but the fog was filling her brain now as well as her senses and she kept putting down her quill absently.

"Oh, and Rector Thomson, of course," Victor said.

He tapped his fingers idly on the tabletop between them, clearly unaware he did so. Lucy dutifully picked up the quill, dipped it in the inkwell, and wrote the rector's name, but then she put the quill down again. She stood suddenly.

Victor gave her an inquiring look, and his fingers stopped their tapping.

"The, uh, the buns tonight," Lucy said, forcing herself not to pace, to stand still behind her chair. She curled her fingers along the top edge of its high back, gripping it tightly. "They were very good. Delicious, in fact. Like the ones we had at the Queens' House."

A smile formed on his face, tugging as a smile always did at the scar near his mouth. But how curious; she recognized that she'd grown used to his scar in the past half month. She'd also grown used to his hard glares when he caught her looking at it. Such a reaction would have offended her once, but not any more. Now, somehow, she knew it was as much bluster as boldness on his part. She thought perhaps she'd pushed aside his last show of boldness when she had asked him if the scar hurt, and he'd run away almost before answering her.

Tonight, though, he was plainly pleased by her assessment of his baking, even if he did not claim it aloud. His smile, which spread clear up into the dark eyes that seemed all pupil in candlelight, proved that. The smile also tugged at her, made tears form in her eyes for a moment before she could blink them away, and made her smile crookedly back at him. It didn't matter that the scar was tugged when he smiled—he had an engaging, inviting smile. It had struck her suddenly, oddly emotionally, that she had too seldom seen it.

"Are you well?" he asked with a quick frown, coming to his feet and moving to her side at once. "Are those tears in your eyes? Why?"

What could she say? That his smile had drawn her tears? She doubted he'd appreciate her curious logic.

She could not tell him that it was more than that, though, that somehow he'd stepped around the barrier between them. He had made her see him not just as a man, with a man's strength and failings, but as one worthy of affection, and truth, and even regard.

God help me, she thought, for she knew a name for that fog that crept into her brain and her vitals, knew by what name to call this feeling of lunacy. She knew it, but could not call it thus to him, not when he remained so clearly unaffected, untouched by it. She knew that her breathing would quicken just because he'd stepped closer to her, just because she could smell the scent of yeast and flour on him yet, just because he was no longer an enemy to her in her heart.

She had come to care for him. In little more than a fortnight, he'd somehow managed to befriend himself to her, even though it once had seemed so unlikely.

If he'd been any other man, she might have tilted back her head, exposing her mouth to him. She might have let nature run its course and seen if a kiss would quiet the chorus in her head or make it sing all the louder.

But he was not any other man. He was the man who had demurred at the meager task of helping her down from her horse, the man who had tensed at the very thought of a simple touch from her.

She could not turn up her mouth to his, could not expose so naked a need, not when she had every expectation he would refuse her.

He stared at her, his gaze shifting slowly down from her eyes to her mouth as if seeking the answer she'd not given him. His gaze rested on her lips, and for one very long moment Lucy thought with a wild joy that he might lean down his head, might press a kiss upon her anyway. She caught her breath and watched his eyes as they lingered on her lips, stunning herself with the strength of longing that gripped her. She wanted to urge him to it, wanted to answer a question she hadn't even known she'd wondered at, wanted what had seemed so impossible only a few minutes ago.

She reached out a hand toward his chest, not entirely sure where she meant to place it; perhaps over his heart or perhaps she meant to grip his waistcoat and pull him to her. Only it did not matter what her intent might have been, for he stepped back, away from her, out of her reach.

She nearly sagged from the calamity of his choice, nearly cried out.

"I know." She gulped out the words, something, anything, some words that might cover her embarrassment, might make it seem she'd been playing at some game. "I know about the baking."

"What?" he said, looking stupefied.

She gave a little gesture with her hand, a false display of nonchalance. "I know that you like to bake bread."

"Oh," he said, shaking his head, then nodding. "Yes. I do." He turned away from her with a little shrug, but not before she'd gotten a glimpse of the frown that had formed on his face. "I like it, the feel of it, the craft of it. What we can't use here, I give away to the tenants. They seem to appreciate it."

Of course he shared the bread with his tenants—she knew now that it was far more like him to share than it had ever been for him to scowl. But she had earned his scowls years ago. She knew she had hurt him, that time he'd overheard her comment about scars. What would she give at this moment to be able to undo that hurt, to erase what had been so unintentionally inflicted on him?

He gave another shrug, turning back to face her. His expression had become hooded, a return to the old cool look that used to be the only one he ever gave her. Her heart squeezed in her chest, and she had to work to keep her lower lip from trembling.

"I suppose my liking to bake bread makes me appear rather common in your eyes," he said accusingly.

It had; he was so right, but he was also so wrong. She fought to find the right words that would undo the last five minutes, the last five years, but there were no such words. His scar had gone several shades of red deeper, an indication of his agitation; her gaze went to it almost without volition.

She should not have allowed it, though. It was exactly the wrong thing; a kind of wrath filled his poor, scarred face, overriding what had only been a wounded displeasure before.

Without stepping back, he still managed to withdraw from the circle of her presence, a pulling away that hurt more than a slap would have done. His mouth formed a snarl, and he spun and stormed out of the room.

Lucy covered her face with shaking hands, too stunned to cry. What had she done? What had happened?

She lowered her hands, her arms feeling boneless. She remained dry-eyed, but not for lack of an agony of regret. She knew what she had done. She knew what she had felt. Attraction, longing, desire . . . *Be honest, girl, and thereby save something of your soul,* she chided herself fiercely. *Call it by its real name: lust.* She'd lusted after Victor, had wanted him to kiss her—*be honest!*—had wanted more than kisses.

She'd taken what ought to have been natural, what should have come with the fullness of time, and like errant steeplechasers had only managed to knock down the very barrier she'd meant to clear. She'd known how he'd reacted to her earlier today, dreading to touch her, and yet had foolishly offered herself to him as though she were some kind of irresistible sweet. If she felt like a confectionery crushed beneath his boot, it was no more than she deserved.

What was to be done? Was there anything that could do aught but make matters worse?

She picked up a candle with shaking hands and moved out of the room to the stairs, climbing them one resigned step at a time. If Victor would talk to her tomorrow, she would tell him that she would go back to London. She would remove her noisome presence from his life. He could stay here, as she supposed he would wish—or the other way around. She'd do as he liked, go where he asked her to go.

She'd never meant to, but she'd hurt him tonight.

Tomorrow she must pay whatever price he asked of her in recompense for her thoughtless cruelties, must forget her attraction and accept his rejection.

She went to bed and waited, sleepless, for tomorrow to come.

Chapter 11

The stables were filled with night aromas, the subtle heated scent of horseflesh at rest, of hay and straw, the grassy scent of dung, the tang of leather. Lucy welcomed the scents, an olfactory reminder that life went on, that the world kept spinning, that all wounds must lose the worst of their sting with time.

The stable lads were asleep in their rooms above the horses. One of them snored loudly enough that Lucy could hear it, but the sound mixed with the occasional shuffling of the horses only added to the comforting familiarity of the place. This was not the Dorcaster mews, but it was much like it, making it a place of solace.

She moved to hang the partially shuttered lamp she'd brought with her on a metal hook designed for that purpose, a safer repository than on a simple peg; one could not be too careful with fire in a stable. The horses were secured with simple leads that allowed them to nibble at their hay and toss their heads or even lie down as they sometimes chose to do. The nearest gelding lifted its head so that one eye could peer at Lucy and her light, but the animal was quickly satisfied that all was well, the great head disappearing once more from sight.

Only a few feet from the hook and lamp there was the remains of a wooden chair. It had lost all accoutrements but its seat and four legs, but Lucy was glad to spy it. She tugged her cloak more tightly around herself, grateful for the warmth it added to her nightrail and wrap, and moved to sit.

She slid a finger into her nightrail's sleeve, pulling free the letter she'd stored there since she had no pockets. It had arrived that morning, and would have been posted at least several days ago. Just the sight of Mama's familiar handwriting on the outside of the folded missive was enough to make her have to blink away tears. Mama, loving as she was, would think Lucy a great peagoose, not only for making Victor think she found his scar unbearable to look upon, but by not disproving that falsehood through the simple expediency of bedding him.

It's not that simple, Lucy thought, as if speaking to her absent mother.

She broke the wafer that sealed the letter closed and unfolded the single page. It was composed in four different hands: Mama's, Papa's, Reuben's, and lastly Rebecca's. How sweet of them all to write at least a little something. Mama inquired after the local events and wrote of some Town gossip; Papa wondered about the weather compared to London's and how the planting of crops was coming along at Oxenby Manor. He added:

So sorry, my girl. I never meant to make a muddle of things. Reuben and I have our heads together, though, and mean to right things. It will be a while, though. I hope you can forgive me for being an old fool.—Papa

Lucy swallowed hard and blinked back more tears, forgiving him in that moment if she hadn't already before.

Reuben wrote:

Money situation not utterly desperate. Less terrible than feared, also less than could have been hoped for. Ah well! The recent good news: seed for this year's crops was paid for in advance, so there will be income eventually, God willing and if the corn grows. Might one day talk of your dowry coming to Oxenby, but for now must concentrate on Rebecca.

Lucy wholeheartedly agreed, for it was evident that neither Victor nor his estate suffered from an empty purse. If she could not apologize to him or somehow make things better between them, he might want her to leave, possibly forever. Although it pained her to think of it, she'd then have to ask him for a yearly allowance. It would help so much if she could bring something with her to negate the costliness of returning to her father's home. She shook her head, sighed deeply, and sent up a little prayer it wouldn't come to that. Forgiveness was a part of marriage, too, was it not? She sighed again and turned her mind back to the letter.

On a seemingly less serious note Reuben mentioned that he was having to chaperone Rebecca all over Town.

Hurry back. I miss Victor's fellowship, and I am wearied unto death of some of the company Rebecca is keeping.

That was peculiar, for Lucy knew that Reuben generally liked Rebecca's beau, Mr. Ellis. Could he mean someone else? Too, it was unlike him to be vague. He'd known that Rebecca was to be given the letter to write upon also, which might explain why he had not been more forthright . . . but, then again, Rebecca could not have appreciated what little he'd already written there for her to see. The more Lucy thought on it, the odder it seemed.

She read on. Rebecca wrote a quick summary of the parties she'd attended that week and what she'd worn, and a few tidbits about some of the young women they both knew, such as Miss Summerall becoming engaged and Lady Philipa Cartwright turning her ankle stepping down wrong from her carriage.

It was what she wrote next that explained Reuben's diffidence.

I have the most delicate question to ask you, dearest Lucianne. It seems I have two suitors. Mr. Ellis is the very dearest of friends to me, but I have another who says he wishes to befriend me. In truth, Lucy, I think he means more than those words say. I think he wishes to court me, but I must have your answer first, as I should not wish to distress you in any way.

Lucy's heart began to pound painfully and she knew the rest before she even read it—but she read it anyway, hoping she was wrong.

Mr. Jerome Holden has paid most particular attention to me of late. I know it is irregular for a man to be betrothed to one sister, and then to another of the same family.

Here Rebecca's handwriting got larger and loopier, a reflection of the agitation she had to be feeling as she wrote.

But I cannot help but think that I should be doing as you have done, a great favor to our family in its recent trying times, by considering a husband who has an income commensurate with family needs. Lucianne, would it be so terrible a thing if I were to allow Mr. Holden to court and marry me?

Springing to her feet, Lucy read the letter over again. She would have paced if not for needing the lamp's light by which to read. She lowered the letter and put one unsteady hand to her mouth.

Clearly Rebecca had been told about the family finances, but that was not what concerned Lucy. *Jerome Holden, courting her sister?* She glanced at the top of the letter, but no one had thought to date it. Still, the news could not be more than a week old. *Jerome was trying to woo Rebecca after little more than a week's separation from herself?*

Clearly Jerome could not be in love with Rebecca, just as he could never have ever really loved Lucy, nor even cared much for her if he was willing to hurt her, hurt both sisters, in this way.

Lucy crumpled the letter and tossed it to the straw-strewn ground, not out of any sense of losing Jerome Holden's love, but out of sheer frustration that she could do nothing about this tonight.

Such a courtship could not go forward. Whatever else she knew, she knew that Jerome did not love Rebecca. There was something of revenge in his actions, she thought. Or perhaps this was a way of salvaging his pride. Or both.

She wanted to be there right now, right this moment, telling Rebecca that the family would do well enough, that Rebecca could not accept a man so undeserving of her sweet nature.

But she could do nothing tonight. She had to wait

until morning, until after she had packed and . . . and until after the discussion she must have with Victor, the apology she hoped he would accept.

She knew she ought to go to her room and try to sleep—but how could she sleep now with all this wretchedness filling her thoughts?

One of the horses nickered softly, its head turned her way, its nostrils flaring as it searched the night air for signs that someone had brought it a treat. Lucy went to the stall where the horse was secured by its leading rope and moved around it to stroke its long nose. "I'm sorry I did not bring a carrot or some bits of apple," she apologized in a whisper, but then she froze, for footsteps were rapidly approaching the stable.

There were two large, wide doors that were presently closed, used to move animals and carriages in and out. To the left of that was a door sized for humans to use. It was that door that was flung open, revealing an agitated male figure holding a candle aloft. It was Victor.

Lucy started to speak his name out of sheer surprise, but then she realized that he had not seen her. She took a step back, letting the horse and shadows hide her. She was not ready to have their conversation, not now.

He was attired in an evening coat hastily thrown over a nightshirt, his feet covered only by house shoes and his ankles exposed to the cold night air. Lucy would have looked away except that her attention was fixed by the relief on his face, which was quickly followed by annoyance. He'd been awake at this late hour—she wondered why. Whatever reason, he'd been awake to see a light in the stables, and he'd come at once, fearing fire of course.

His expression would have been comical under

other circumstances, because at the same time he was clearly appeased at finding no fire and exasperated that someone had left a lamp burning untended.

She saw him glance overhead, no doubt thinking of rousting the grooms from their beds for a scolding. He crossed to take the lamp from its hook, but in midmotion he paused.

Her heart sank as she saw him bend and lift her crumpled letter from the ground. He put his candle on the chair and smoothed the letter with both hands, only then taking up the candle once more and holding it near the letter. He read for only a few moments, but then he jerked the letter down and away, ceasing to read it as he stared straight ahead, a puzzled frown turning down the corners of his mouth.

Lucy gave a small gasp as unexpected equine lips gummed her hand, the horse evidently still hopeful that a treat would be forthcoming. Her tiny gasp was enough, however, to secure Victor's gaze, which riveted on her despite the darkness. It took him only two seconds more to recognize her. "Lucy!"

Her heart did a strange flip. He'd always called her by her full name before, and the shortened "Lucy" felt strangely intimate in this unlooked-for moment.

"I . . . I couldn't sleep," she said, not adding the hurtful "under your roof."

She was acutely aware that her hair hung in two long plaits and that she wore only her night things under her cloak, but she thought perhaps the cloak did a lot to disguise her undress. Not that Victor was any the finer in his attire than she, being most obviously in his night things.

She could hardly linger in the dark, though, now that she'd been discovered. She moved away from the horse and the shadows, just a few steps that scarcely brought her closer to Victor but put her into the circle of light the lamp threw.

"I guess I wanted company." She gestured back toward the horses, hearing with her own ears how idiotic the statement sounded.

He stared at her for a long moment, then down at the paper in his hand. "Your letter," he said, holding it up, making it possible for her to see that his hand trembled.

"Victor?" Why should his hand tremble so? she wondered.

"I never meant to read it. I didn't read it, not really. Just a few sentences, but then I realized it was yours and I stopped—" A small frown formed between his eyes. "I am sorry," he said with a kind of stiff dignity, extending the letter toward her. "I truly did not mean to read your private missive."

"I know," she said, stepping close enough to accept the letter. "I saw that you stopped when you realized what it was."

He nodded, not looking particularly gratified by her acknowledgment. "It is cold out here. Come," he said, taking one step back toward the stable door, "let us return to the house."

"Of course." She'd look the perfect idiot to demur, but she did so anyway. "I'll be along in a minute or two."

"I'd rather you went up to the house with me now."

"I'll bring the lamp—you don't have to worry about that," she assured him. He looked . . . odd, upset. He could not like it that with each thing she said, she sounded more and more like an imbecile.

"I know you would bring the lamp," he said, sounding exasperated. "I just don't want to . . . I don't like the idea of leaving a lady alone in a stable."

Now it was her turn to stare. "Are you concerned about footpads, do you mean? So far out from Colchester?" She thought that highly unlikely and started to shake her head.

"Not footpads!" His tone was harsher than it needed to be. He must be all out of patience with her; certainly he was trembling all over now. "Just come. Now. Please."

"Victor!" she said, caught between being exasperated herself and a little alarmed. His "please" had been wrung out of him as if he were under torture. "Do you have a fever? You are shaking so."

Victor reached out and grabbed her wrist, not hard but firmly, and pulled her to the stable door. He yanked the door open, pushed her unceremoniously out into the yard, and followed a long moment later holding both the candle and the lamp.

He watched the door just long enough to see it swing closed behind him, then lowered his chin to his chest, his eyes closed as though he were in pain. He stood very still except for the too-rapid rise and fall of his chest and the unsteadiness of the flames he held in shaking hands.

Slowly his trembling subsided, and his posture relaxed. He lifted his head and met her eye, astonishing her with a sheepish look. "I'm sorry," he apologized a second time tonight. "I had no right to be rough with you. I pray I haven't hurt you."

She shook her head, not releasing his gaze, keeping it fixed with her own. "Victor," she said slowly, now stepping closer to him the better to note his widened eyes, the perspiration on his upper lip, the shocking paleness of his skin even under the golden glow of lamplight. "Victor, what is wrong?"

"Nothing," he said, the sound little more than a low growl.

"Are you ill?"

"No."

She made a little gesture with her head, a tiny shake that denied he was telling the truth and reflected her sudden desire to shake him. "Is there something in the stables I should not know about?"

"No!" This denial, at last, sounded real. "I just—" He stopped and gave a short, sharp shake of his head. His lips stretched into a grimace, and he let out a sudden hard sigh. "You might as well know, even though you'll think me the greatest fool in the world. Some of my servants know. Reuben knows."

"Knows what?" He was frightening her a little.

The sheepish look came over him again, but it served to calm her alarm. "I'm fairly certain you do not have a secret society or smugglers meeting here," she said, but her feeble attempt at humor did not touch him.

"I do not like horses."

She laughed, and he scowled, and she realized immediately that she'd erred.

"Victor!" she said. "Whatever can you mean? That you are *afraid* of horses?"

"That is exactly what I mean," he said, his voice deepened by some emotion she could only guess at. He turned and began walking toward the house.

She hurried to catch up to him, his longer stride forcing her to all but run. "You cannot mean that! That is like being afraid of . . ." She fumbled for an example. "Of trees! They are everywhere, they are a part of life."

He stopped, turning abruptly to face her. "A part I am disinclined to enjoy. Or even tolerate well," he ground out. She met him stare for stare, and saw that he meant what he said.

He made a disgusted noise, then spun toward the house. She noticed that his limp was more pronounced when he hurried.

She caught up to him again as he gave her a quick sideways glance.

"The doctors call it a form of mania," he said, still walking, now staring straight ahead. " 'Temporary onset of mania stimulated by exposure to equines' is what they call it, which sounds so much nicer than saying I fall into fits of insanity. I'd protest, except it's true enough. Around horses I feel . . . sensations of dread. Sometimes I can keep command of my senses if I step away in time, yet other times . . ." He fell silent, his scowl only lending to the fierceness of his scar.

Lucy fell silent as well, walking beside him, pondering what he obviously felt to be true. It was easy to see how such a fear could have come upon him; one had only to look at his scar and limp and know how he'd received them, to understand. One of the children living on her street in London had been bitten by a dog last year, and the child was deathly afraid of all dogs now, even crying just at the sound of distant barking. But Victor was a man grown—and yet a dread of horses explained so much.

It explained why he walked so much, even in the country where distances tended to discourage walking over riding. It explained why he never drove himself, always leaving the horses to be handled by a coachman; why he looked uncomfortable in a carriage; why he'd stepped away from her and the horse she'd been riding earlier today; why he had gone pale and shaky in the stables, mere feet from the hooved creatures.

He'd not wanted her to remain in the stables, in his estimation too near dangerous beasts. His fear had not been just for himself, but for her safety. It was rather flattering if one looked at it that way. Lucy felt a warm glow that was quite at contrast with the cool March evening air.

"I did not know," she said in apology.

He gave another grimace, which might have been an attempt at a self-deprecating smile. "Good. I am encouraged, thinking that perhaps I've managed to keep the whole world from knowing."

She put her hand on his arm, the simple gesture proving enough to stop his forward flight. He turned to face her, his look guarded.

"You needn't go then, of course. I would hate to distress you further," she said.

"Go where?"

"To London. You can stay here, and I will be the one to leave if you wish me to go. Victor, earlier tonight . . . I owe you an apology for all that happened, but I'll . . . I'll understand if it is not enough, or if you need me to leave here for a while, or—"

"Leave? Why are you leaving?" She thought she heard a measure of upset in his tone, and felt very perverse at being gratified to hear it, pleased that the idea of her leaving affected him.

"I'm sorry," she said, realizing she really was a fool for not at least giving him the chance to accept her apology, for presuming he could not forgive her for her unkindnesses. "I know I hurt you, but, Victor, I truly had not meant to, and I am truly sorry. I know I shouldn't have . . . I acted very forward, I know it now. And I understand perfectly that you . . . that I am not the woman you would have wished to marry—"

"Lucy," he interrupted, making her stomach flip

again with the use of her shortened name. "What are you on about?"

She looked away, confused by his odd expression. He did not look angry or disgusted, but certainly agitated. She could not imagine what he was thinking, for she was making such a hash of her apology.

She sighed, tucked her cloak more tightly around herself, and began again. "I have thought that you might wish me to leave Oxenby Manor . . . for a while. You would stay here, of course, especially now that I know that traveling by carriage is not your favorite activity."

"Lucianne," he said, and although he'd chosen the formal version of her name, there was so much of injury in his voice that it struck her even more deeply than the pet name had. She looked up at him, feeling her own face fill with distress in response to the hurt, puzzled look on his face.

"Is this because I was angry earlier? Lucianne, you must have a thicker hide than that, surely? Surely a few acrimonious words are not enough to send you flying from me, from this marriage? If I'd had any idea . . ."

He tried to keep a scowl from his brow, but he succeeded only in looking wounded. "We Oxenbys are a common sort, given to pride and temper, but I assure you that I can better control myself if it is distressing to you." The last was asked as a question, the answer to which he awaited while letting her see the anxiety in his gaze.

She could not turn her face away from his, for he would misunderstand that. He would think that she disliked his openness, his willingness to let her see his bewilderment. But she could close her eyes, at least long enough to tamp down the anguish that rose into them along with tears.

Merciful heavens, she realized the man was taking the blame for their little scene earlier on himself! He was playing the gallant, ignoring how she'd all but thrown herself at him, that it had been her fault that tension had spiraled between them. It had been her eyes that had gone to his scar, had made him feel marred or lacking or both. He had nothing to apologize for, and yet he did so.

Another thought occurred to Lucy, a thought so unexpected and so strangely welcome that it brought her eyes open so that she could examine his face. She saw the scar, of course, but it was unimportant, insignificant. What she really searched for, she found, and the finding of it made her heart sing: He did not want her to go. Whatever his reason, he was not ready to give up on their marriage, was not wholly repulsed by her. It might all be duty, it might all be his living up to a commitment—but his pledge bound him still all the same.

"You're wrong, Victor," she said, seeing a new hurt begin to form in his eyes at the words, so she hurried to say more. "There is nothing common about the Oxenbys, nothing at all."

The hurt retreated, leaving at first a wary look in his eyes, which slowly formed into an uncertain smile. She saw the hesitant smile retreat and return twice, and then she saw the new question in his eyes.

"You'll stay?" he asked.

She shook her head, fumbling with her sleeve to retrieve the letter she'd restored there. "I have to go to London. Read all of this, and you'll know why. But, Victor, I am . . . content not to go there alone." *Content?* It was too little a word, but any other word said too much, exposed too much. He was noble, this husband of hers, Lucy could form no doubt of that, but it did not mean he was in love with her.

Love? What a wondrous, devastating word. A day ago it had been a word she thought she knew all about, a thing she thought she'd experienced in all its dimensions. But tonight, if she knew nothing else, she knew she'd been an innocent little fool with eyes closed.

Her eyes were wide open now, no longer blind to a very simple truth: She loved Victor.

At the realization, her heart sang and her stomach plummeted. The one sensation was deliciously intoxicating, the other agonizing. She was in love with the man to whom she was married—but only God knew if Victor could ever come to love her.

He looked up from the letter he'd just read. "I will go with you," he said firmly.

She could have told him he need not torture himself with a carriage ride, but she did not. She merely nodded, unable to speak for the lump in her throat, put there by the thought that he'd suffer for the sake of being with her. It did not matter what motivated his wishing to be there, only that he had chosen not to let her go away, alone.

"We can pack in the morning and still be on our way soon enough," he said now, his low voice making her shiver, but not from the cold. "You should find your bed."

She nodded. Victor offered her his arm, and together they continued the few remaining steps to the front door of the house.

Keeping her hand on his arm, Lucy was led across the hall and up the stairs. She did not take her hand away until he stopped before her door. She nodded again, unable even to murmur good night before turning to slip quietly into her room.

She waited just on the other side of the closed door until she heard the shuffled retreat of his house shoes and the hushed sound of his own door being closed. She stood, leaning on the door several heartbeats longer, then crossed to her mantel. She slid the key into the lock of the door between their rooms and turned it, releasing the locking mechanism with a soft click.

Returning the key to the mantel, she saw her hand was shaking a little where it touched the wooden surface. She leaned forward, for a long minute allowing her forehead to rest against the back of her hand. It was a prayerlike attitude, which suited well enough, for she vowed silently that she would do nothing to hurt Victor further.

He had been nothing but courtly with her, and she owed him as much in return. She could—she *would* mind her emotions; she would return his gentility with the best deportment she could summon. It didn't matter what her wants or desires were—she would return Victor's gallantries with genteel decorum of her own. She would be a good wife to him, even if she was never the wife of his heart.

She crossed to her bed, tearless and determined, even if her lower lip trembled. She was glad she was already in her night things, that she need not ring for a maid, for a maid would surely see the heightened emotions that lingered in her gaze.

Chapter 12

As their coach pulled away from yet another tollgate, Victor gave a sigh of relief. Tollgates at midday were often exactly as they'd found this one to be: crowded, dusty, and filled with ill-tempered travelers. Their coachman had been forced to jostle through a crowd, and the proximity of all that horseflesh had made Victor's palms turn cold and clammy. It took only one horse to bolt or rear, and then there would be a half dozen collisions among carriages or someone afoot would be run over or . . .

He forced his breathing to slow, reminding himself that the toll was paid, and the crowd quickly falling behind them. He glanced out of the corners of his eyes toward Lucy. Was he glad he'd told her his secret? He'd managed over the years to keep most people from knowing about it—it felt odd to know that Lucy knew. And yet, he no longer had to pretend to be at ease as they drove. Not having to pretend made it that much easier to bear, oddly enough.

Telling her had not cured him; he was under no such illusion, but not having to hide it from her left him with that much more ability to endure.

He could openly hold the carriage strap when the road became uneven, and he need not make idle chatter during the worse passages. He was free to rap on the roof, a reminder to the coachman to slow the horses' pace, although he tried to avoid doing it in order not to make the journey that much longer for Lucianne.

Lucianne—she'd asked him to accompany her to London, and he'd said he would go. He might have more closely examined the reason why he'd made that choice, except the carriage ride itself interfered with more rational thought, or so he explained the nameless, formless feelings that had compelled him to accompany his bride back to London.

Just when it seemed the road had evened out again, one of the carriage wheels dipped into a deep hole, jolting the coach and its occupants. Victor reached with both hands for the carriage strap, feeling perspiration bead at once on his forehead and upper lip. The jolt was followed with another and then another, and then careful breathing was not enough anymore. He felt the old, hated sinking feeling; the mania was on him again.

It was a thing that wrapped inside his head, that tangled rational thought, leaving little room for anything but reaction, the burning desire for escape. He closed his eyes, he opened them again, he tried to block out the sound of horse hooves, but it was all he could hear.

He knew the feeling so well, too well, and he clung to the one hope he'd had for so long: that the doctors were more wrong than right. If he were truly mad, surely he could have no rational thought, no control, and his world would be forever disintegrating. But his world was well enough so long as he avoided the nearness of horses.

The doctors said he had a mania, and most of them said he would get worse with time, but a few had said they'd seen much the same reaction in some soldiers. Men so afflicted had but to hear a whistle to be suddenly ducking and running, fearing the fall of cannonballs. A sudden crack could make them shake with the memory of rifles firing all around them. Even something as ordinary as a shout could cause some men to fall to the ground, or cry, or scream, or run. They were in all other respects perfectly rational men—except for those moments when memory blocked out reason.

Victor clung to those words, those assessments. Even in the midst of his paroxysms there was a small, discerning part of his brain that knew he'd be right again in a while. He reached for that belief now and fought to swallow down the sense of horror. He clawed at the spiraling panic, tearing it apart, struggling to push it out of his burning brain.

A hand touched his, cool and part of something else, something good, something to be hoped for. A voice reached his ears, sliding past the deadly sound of hooves. He welcomed the voice and reached out nearly blind, folding the hand inside both of his own. Rationality slowly crept back.

His chin was on his chest; he felt he hardly had the strength to lift his head, so he gazed up at Lucy through his eyelashes. It was her hand, her voice that had reached out to him, of course. "Lucy!" he said, his voice little more than a whisper.

"Are you well?"

"Well enough."

"Has it gotten worse over the years?" She sat back, her hand sliding free of his.

He didn't even try to dissemble. "No. I think it is better actually. For the first two years after the accident I couldn't even ride in a carriage at all." He looked down at his hands, which he had folded before him; they were still shaking a little from reaction. He gave a little laugh. "Today being the exception."

She smiled softly, not laughing at him, but accepting his pale humor.

"I know it doesn't make sense," he said, closing his eyes for a moment. "The horse I was holding was not harnessed to a carriage. It was standing still, until it reared of course. It makes a kind of sense that I should dislike horses when I stand near them, but when they are merely pulling a carriage?"

"It is the roughness of the road that alarms you the most," Lucy pointed out.

He opened his eyes to look at her, to concentrate on her face and not his own words. "When the carriage lurches, it reminds me of falling. That's what I remember most about the accident, the sense of being flung to the ground, so suddenly, so . . . ruthlessly. I didn't even hurt at first. I just was dashed to the ground. Then the beast came down on me again, and I felt my leg shatter, and I heard the horse's cry." He gave a sniff of a laugh, with nothing of amusement in it. "That's an odd word to use, but that's how I remember it, the horse crying out. Now I know the animal was probably doing its best not to step on me, but at the time its whinny was . . . it was like laughter, as if it were amused by what it had done."

He shook his head, his mouth twisting into a grimace. "What a half-witted fool I must sound to you."

Lucianne did him the favor of not instantly refuting his words, instead considering them. After a length she said, "You know my sister, Rebecca?"

Victor nodded, perplexed.

"Every year at Christmas our family has performed a mummer's tale, with all of us taking parts. We perform for our cousins and friends and the servants, and anyone else who might be at hand for the season. And every year, just before she steps forth to play her part, poor Rebecca, well"—Lucy blushed at the word—"she retches. She cannot help herself. She gets so nervous. Once she is playing her part, she is well enough, but before then she has her little difficulty."

"It is not quite the same thing," Victor protested, but all the same he felt an odd flood of warmth lace through his veins.

"Is it not? I cannot think why. For just as Rebecca manages to perform her part, you manage to ride in a carriage, do you not?"

Victor met her gaze, wondering if she could see in his own how much he wanted to be persuaded by her. "Some doctors," he said, picking his words carefully, "assure me that it is possible to get better with time. They say I'll never be *tranquil* around horses, but that I can learn to quell the attacks of mania. I've half believed them, sometimes."

Lucy nodded. "Learn to tolerate carriages," she said, her tone firm but kind, "and never ride. That would be my advice."

Victor looked back down at his hands—more steady than they had been—and just managed to keep a foolish grin from forming. Lucy, it seemed, did not find him unduly craven. Words such as "stalwart" or "brave" might not come to her mind, but neither did she utterly disdain the cross he bore.

"Did you get a return missive from the dressmaker before we left Oxenby Manor?" he asked, purposefully changing the subject.

"No, but Mrs. Raleigh assured me she would have the dresses sent on to London at your mama's home."

He listened as Lucy detailed other last-minute directions she'd arranged with Mrs. Raleigh, letting the normal chatter pour over him, soothe him, distract him. He nodded when he ought and murmured when he agreed, and thought to himself that Lucy ought to have even finer gowns than those a country dressmaker could manage. He must be sure more were ordered, now that they were returning to London, including bonnets and gloves and anything else she desired.

It flashed through his mind that he wished she desired him, but he had no illusions that he was the man of her dreams. She'd been compelled to marry him, and she had his promise that he'd wait on her asking for him. She'd seen him in his own kitchens, playing the commoner far better than he played the lord of the manor; she knew his family's ignoble beginnings. She'd seen his dread of horses, of course, and that could hardly inspire a woman's desire.

It did not signify that her presence in his home, in his life, at his side, was slowly filling his head with intoxicating thoughts. It did not matter that a simple smile or a casual gesture from her could suddenly set his blood to coursing. If he burned at night, alone in a lonely bed, it was no fault of hers.

Somehow they had become friends—he knew that today if not before. Her patience, her understanding, her sympathy that was real without being maudlin—these were the traits of a friend. He would follow to her bed in a minute, should she say but one word of invitation. It was even his right as her husband to insist, but not as her friend. To truly be her friend he had to keep his word and await the lady's preference, even though her preference might be never to lie with him.

"Why are you laughing?" she asked him now.

He covered his face with one hand, his shoulders shaking with mirth, shaken to his core by the possibilities he pondered. He could do naught *but* laugh, even though his sudden amusement might serve only to make Lucy find him even that much more peculiar a fellow.

"I was picturing the look on your father's face"—he chose a lesser truth—"if he were to find me baking bread in his kitchens."

"I'd join you," Lucy said, smiling. "It looked like a curative, for relieving sensations of misfortune. I have a feeling I will be needing such a restorative."

He grinned back at her, even as he wondered if she would be able to persuade her sister to have nothing to do with Jerome Holden. But no, he would not, he told himself as he buried a frown, be jealous of the man who had once been the repository of Lucy's affection—but neither would he play the absent husband. He'd be at her side, not least because it was well and away time he began the campaign to woo his own wife.

He knew she did not hate him, something he'd been unsure of before today. Yes, she would have to ask him to her bed, as he'd promised, but why could he not help her along in making that choice?

Lucy stared at the portmanteaux that littered the floor of her room at Dorcaster House. Not only were her boxes there, but Victor's as well. Mama had ordered one room readied for the two of them.

"I assumed they would put you in with Reuben again," Lucy said, her voice flat with shock.

"We have been married for more than two weeks now," Victor pointed out.

Of course Mama assumed we were intimate, Lucy thought with a sinking heart. *It should be true.* "I will talk with her— "

Victor merely gave her a long look, one that spoke volumes.

"Oh!" she said, the sound close to a moan. He was

right, of course. Mama would be horrified to learn her daughter had yet to do her duty. Lucy tossed her bonnet on the nearby table as she sank into a chair before the fireplace. "Explaining to Mama would almost be worse than actually—" She glanced up at Victor, belatedly realizing she could hardly claim sleeping with him would be worse than revealing that she hadn't. "I mean to say—"

"I can sleep in your dressing room," he said, his grimace showing his displeasure at the thought.

Lucy gave a short nod, then slumped back in the chair. "What a day this has been! First Rebecca isn't even here, and now having to share this room—"

"I don't snore." He sounded offended, but another quick glance showed her that he was not truly angry. She thought his half smile might be more resigned than actively resentful.

He moved to sit as well. "When is Rebecca expected to return home?"

"In three days. I cannot believe we came all the way to London only to find she's gone to Brighton with Eliza's family." Eliza Crawford was Rebecca's dearest friend.

"It is only three days. You can talk with her when she returns."

"I hope that is not too late." Was Jerome also in Brighton? she wondered. She certainly did not put it past him to have followed Rebecca there. She sat forward in her chair, suddenly anxious. "Do you think we should go to Brighton and talk to her there?"

"No. Rebecca would not appreciate it, I feel sure, to say nothing of the fact you were not invited."

"But what if Mr. Holden is there with her?"

"She wrote for your permission to allow him to pay her his addresses, remember? She would not act without it."

Lucy was not so sure. She knew from personal experience that Jerome could be persuasive—and Rebecca would be feeling vulnerable right now, knowing that her dowry was spare if not wholly gone, that she had an opportunity to help her family. "What if we wait, but we're wrong, and she comes home engaged?"

"Don't make me say it," he said. He'd taken a light tone, and the almost smile on his mouth invited her to join him in not worrying.

"Don't make you say what?" she asked, allowing the mood in the room to shift.

"That she can become unengaged, just as her older sister did."

Lucy threw him a dark look, and for a moment he looked concerned that he'd insulted her. "Sirrah, I must protest your use of the word 'older,' " she said archly.

He grinned, just as she'd intended he do.

Something had happened between them in the carriage earlier, although she could not think what it might have been. He'd suffered one of his episodes, but that could not have wrought a change, surely? Still, a change had taken place, one that made it possible for them to have a bit of sport without immediate fear of offering each other offense. She was not foolish enough to put it down to love. Her feelings were unrequited—he'd told her as much.

Two weeks ago, whispered a sly voice in her head.

No, she would not allow such thoughts, she determined fiercely. God save her if Victor never came to love her yet learned that she loved him. He could not know. It was one thing to have a marriage of convenience, of mutual benefit, but quite another to burden him with unwanted, unreturned emotions.

A bell—big as a man's head and deeply toned—

rang out from its position near the bottom of the stairs. "Supper will be served on the hour," Lucy explained to Victor's raised eyebrows.

"I will dress in there," he said, indicating the dressing room. He stood and crossed to one of the portmanteaux, lifting it easily to carry it to the small adjoining room.

He returned almost at once, however, looking vexed.

"Is something amiss?"

"Worrell is not here yet." He stated a fact she already knew, since the valet had been set to follow them with more boxes the following day, after he'd had additional time to pack. "I cannot pull my right boot off by myself," he explained, shifting his weight from one foot to the other in apparent agitation. "I can get it on, but not off. I need to ring for a footman."

"Oh," she said. She started to move to the bellpull near her bed, then hesitated, annoyed that color began to bloom in her face at the offer that occurred to her. "I can ring for someone, or I could help you with that myself." It would only take a moment; it was silly, she thought, to ring for a footman when she could do it.

He parted his lips to say something, only to close them again. He nodded, then moved to sit in the nearest chair, his right foot forward.

She'd pulled off her own half boots after riding or walking many a time, but always from a different angle, of course. She bent down and took up his boot in both hands at his ankle, then realized she'd be better off with a different grip, cupping the back of the heel with one hand and the calf of the boot with the other. One tug showed her why it might be difficult for him, since the boots were well fitted, molding his legs. She knew Reuben often had difficulty getting his own boots off as well, and he did not have to contend with an aching limb.

She made a mental note that when they returned to Oxenby Manor, she would order that a bootjack be secured to the floor of his bedchamber. Then if Worrell was not at hand, Victor would have another option for removing his boot, which she could only imagine he would appreciate.

The boot came free on the third try. Lucy stood upright, hoisting it in front of her like a prize fish. Victor rose hastily, his action bringing them very close to each other, only the thickness of the boot between them. His hands came up gripping her elbows as if she might have been pitched backward by his movement, but instead his action only served to pull her closer against him, gown to breeches. Lucy looked up with a teetering smile, one that faded away in degrees marked by the suddenly heavy beating of her heart.

She gazed into his eyes—they were dark, dark brown, like his hair, hair that invited touch. She wanted to run her fingers through it, wanted to feel what her eyes caressed. She was keenly aware how far she had to look up to see his hair, his eyes, his mouth—and just how far away his mouth was from hers.

There was a brief knock at her chamber door, and then her maid hurried in.

"Oh, beg pardon!" the servant exclaimed, clearly surprised to find the occupants of the room standing so close.

Lucy immediately stepped back from Victor. She thrust the boot at him, more tossing it than handing it. She spun so that her back was presented to both Victor and the maid, hoping she'd moved quickly enough to hide the rush of color to her face.

She heard Victor murmur something to the maid, then walk away in one boot and one stocking. She heard him close the door to the dressing room. Only then could she turn to face the maid.

Alice, however, seemed to find nothing amiss with what she'd witnessed. She'd been Lucy's lady's maid since her mistress had left the schoolroom. Had Alice been willing Lucy would have had her come to Essex, but she had chosen to stay on at Dorcaster House. With the ease of long service, Alice quickly fell to chatting.

"Are you liking married life then, Lady Oxenby?" Alice asked as she helped tie the tapes of Lucy's dinner dress.

"Yes."

"Ooh, it does make me laugh to call you that, 'Lady Oxenby.' You've been 'Lady Lucy' so long to me, it fair makes my head spin to think of you as a married lady. Do you like Essex then?"

"Yes."

The maid accepted more of Lucy's unelaborated answers without question, and happily went on to share tidbits of how the household had fared since her lady had gone to the country.

Lucy would have liked to linger in the comforting routine, except Victor had no way out of the dressing room other than into her bedchamber, and it was hardly kind to make him wait unduly. She dismissed Alice and went to tap on the door. "Victor? You may come out if you're ready."

She moved away at once, crossing the room to stand beside the door to the corridor, far from any accidental touch. Victor came from the room, his boots replaced by dark leather shoes. He was wearing dark trousers instead of breeches. Lucy looked away. She'd certainly seen trousers before, on Reuben even if Papa did not care for the fashion, and every day on the streets and in the parks of London. But the length of them made Victor seem that much taller and accentuated the musculature she'd noted while helping him with his boot. The look was very . . . flattering.

Pulling the door open with haste, Lucy led the way down to supper.

Normally she would have enjoyed both the meal and the accompanying tattle, especially since she'd been gone for over a fortnight. However, she soon had her fill of both the repast and the recounting of recent gossip and rumored exploits. She felt restless and skitterish. She thought she must be anxious to talk to Rebecca, plus it had been a long day, one full of disturbances. She was not exactly anxious for the awkwardness of going to bed this night, but the idea of being tucked under warm blankets, perhaps with a book to read for a little while until she felt sleepy, was attractive.

"Oxenby, will you take port with Reuben and me?" Papa offered as he at last pushed away from the table.

"Gladly," Victor answered.

Lucy watched the three men leave to seek Papa's book room, and wondered how many bottles of spirits remained in the cool dirt pit dug in a corner of the kitchens. Enough for tonight anyway, clearly. She suspected the men would put their heads together over the matter of Dorcaster finances while they sipped at their snifters, and perhaps Victor would offer to help.

How curious that now she thought it likely he would make such an offer. A month before he might have done so for Reuben's sake, but he'd have thought twice knowing that Lucy would benefit as well. That had changed—as the queen had said, there was power in the two simple words "I do."

Regardless of how the men spent their time over their port, Lucy knew an opportunity when it presented itself. She said an early good night to her mama, determined to go up to bed, change into her night things, and get settled long before Victor came up.

She was contentedly under the covers, a book at hand and two candelabra providing enough light for reading, when something awkward occurred to her.

"Alice," she called, stopping the maid just before she could slip out the door, "you needn't come back tonight. Lord Oxenby and I will tend the fire."

"Very good, m'lady," the maid said, unable to suppress a knowing smile.

"Oh, and wait for our ring in the morning," Lucy added, clinging to dignity despite the maid's obvious interpretation of her instructions.

"Yes, ma'am," Alice said on a poorly smothered giggle just before she curtsied her way out.

Lucy heaved a sigh and fanned her bright red face for a few moments. Well, that *was* the impression they meant to give the servants, she supposed.

The bed, that infamous symbol of marital unity, was warm and it invited her to remain, but she had to rise from it all the same. There was no point in being settled before Victor came up if at that time they had to decide what his sleeping arrangements would be. Better to prepare them now.

It was a thing done easily enough. A pillow from the bed, several blankets from the clothespress . . . "That is not enough," she mused aloud. She carried the items to the dressing room, settling them on the bit of carpet there, then returned to her bedchamber to fetch the counterpane from her bed. She might be a little cold without it, but at least she was in a room with a fireplace, unlike Victor. If she got cold, she'd probably wake enough to actually maintain the coals all night, as she had claimed she'd do.

Everything settled, including new coal on the fire, she returned to her bed and her book. It was a bit difficult to concentrate on the story, but she put down any remaining restlessness to the uniqueness of waiting for a man to pass through her bedroom.

A knock on the door came sooner than she'd expected. Her call of "Come in!" resulted in affirming it was Victor who had knocked.

"Lucianne." He stood just inside the closed door, offering her a rather formal nod of the head.

"Victor," she responded in kind.

She'd admired his form clad in trousers before, and a second glimpse did nothing to change her opinion. The dim light from her candles did much to hide his scar, giving her a glimpse of what his face would have been had it remained unmarked. He was striking, make no mistake. In fact, in full light it was seeing the handsome half of his face that made the scar that much more unfortunate.

But does it matter? a small voice in her head asked. Was the man not so much more than his scar? His limp? Even his fear of horses? She knew all these things of him—and yet she loved him.

He glanced toward the dressing room.

"I've placed blankets and a pillow in there for you," she assured him.

"Ah! Well then, good night."

"Good night. Do take a candle with you."

He crossed to light a single candle from one of her candelabra, then gave her a little bow. As he walked to the dressing room, she had to swallow a giggle at the silliness of their formality with each other. Were they not in a bedchamber and in various stages of dress, their manners could have suited perfectly well for Hyde Park.

She read for a while before blowing out her candles, but despite the warmth and the dark, sleep did not come.

She got up once to pour a glass of water from the ewer on the side table, sucking in her breath at the touch of the chilly floor. She got up another time to replenish the coals, again struck by the evening's chill.

When she still could not sleep, both the cold and guilt had begun to gnaw at her. She was cold, and yet she was in the room with heat. Victor must be freezing.

This was ridiculous.

She rose from the bed and crept to his door, knocking quietly.

"Yes?" came his voice at once. "Lucy? Are you all right?"

She started to ask if she might open the door, but before she could he had pulled it open. Even in the meager light cast by the coals she could see that he wore only his nightshirt, apparently eschewing or having no access to a nightcap. His hair was mussed, but his features did not have the look of interrupted sleep about them. Had he been unable to find slumber also? she wondered.

"Lucy?" he repeated.

She did so like the sound of her name when he said it. And he never called her "Elf."

"I'm quite well," she assured him, speaking quietly. "It is just . . ." She hurried on, before she could change her mind. "I have noticed how cold it is, and I cannot think you must be warm in this closet. I think you should come out and sleep by the fire."

He thought about it a moment, then nodded. "I shouldn't mind the heat, I must confess," he now also spoke low.

"Good. It is settled them."

He moved to scoop up his bed things. She started to retreat, but then she saw he had dropped something. She could not tell it was the pillow until she'd entered the unlighted room and put her hand on it. "Is there anything else?"

"I've got the blankets," he told her, leading the way out of the room.

Chapter 13

Victor glanced around her bedchamber and decided that an arrangement at the end of the bed would suit best.

"If I settled right before the coals, I might well catch myself on fire. And this way I won't block all the heat from reaching you," he explained.

He spread the blankets so that half would be under him and half over, dropping the pillow at one end of the folded arrangement. He used the coal shovel to throw more fuel on the fire, then turned to nod to Lucy. "Thank you."

She tried to smile, but she suddenly felt like the biggest peagoose. What elaborate game was this she was playing? Why all this foolishness?

"I am ridiculous," she said, her voice roughened by a sudden surge of tears at the back of her throat.

"What? Why?" he asked, just as she ought to have known he would. She shouldn't have said anything. He dipped one shoulder, trying to look into her face.

"I am your wife, but . . . but look! I am making you sleep on the floor, like a dog at the foot of my bed."

"I wouldn't be the first husband so treated," he said, still trying to catch her eye, but only succeeding long enough to let her glimpse a wry smile.

"I am not behaving properly—"

"Really? I'd say things were a bit *too* proper."

She gave a watery giggle, despite herself. "That is not what I meant."

"I know." He straightened up and put a hand under her elbow. "Come on then, back to bed. You're tired, and today was very frustrating, and you need your rest."

She let him lead her to the bed, let him tuck her under the blankets. He was a good man, the best of men. He had every right to take advantage of the situation, every right to demand a warm bed, and yet he waited on her welcome.

He surprised her by leaning down and planting a hand on either side of her head. He leaned forward to place a kiss on her forehead. "I am not anyone named Nanny, but I hope that is enough to let you sleep now," he said with a soft smile.

She put her hand on his arm before he could pull away. She watched his eyelids half close, that hooded look of his that told her nothing of his thoughts.

She searched for words, but the only ones that came close to suiting were too simple. "Thank you," she said anyway.

He, too, seemed unable to find the correct words, settling on a nod instead.

He lingered a moment longer, which was enough for Lucy to reach up, to respond to a sudden and nearly irresistible impulse. Despite the uneven shadows cast by the coal fire, she saw the beginnings of a beard and mustache on his face, and she saw where the scarred skin bore no hint of hair.

Victor grew very still, perhaps not breathing. Lucy thought perhaps she forgot to breathe as well, but breath was unimportant at the moment. It was enough that her fingers traced where her eyes looked, confirming what she saw. It was enough that Victor allowed her to trace the entire length of his scar.

She looked away from the scar, into his eyes, and realized that to have touched him there was an intimacy beyond mere flesh. Doctors may have touched his wound, his mama perhaps—but no sweetheart or strumpet ever had. He did not need to tell Lucy for her to know it for a truth. He did not need to tell her that, as public as its display had to be, his scar was the most private part of his body.

He had not chided her for daring to touch him there, nor stopped her.

Oh, Victor.

She put her hands on either side of his head and pulled his mouth down to hers. They kissed, a short and simple kiss, but when he raised his mouth from hers, she did not see a question in his gaze. He knew. She had invited him, and he knew it. She had vowed never to hurt him again, and she knew that to send him away from her bed this night would be to hurt him. He could take her maidenhead, but she had taken something far more costly from him, and she would not betray that trust. She had vowed not to, nor did she want to. She slid from under his arms, inching over in the bed, making room for him.

As he crawled under the blankets beside her, the light caught a pulse in his neck, a cadence to match her own pounding heart.

He leaned over her, kissing her again. She liked his kiss, and felt a strange quickening at the idea of receiving more.

"What do you know?" he pulled back to ask gently.

She did not pretend to misunderstand. "Enough. I've seen animals. Reuben told me some things when we were younger and less . . . aware of discretion. Mama tried to tell me something before we left for

Essex." She could not meet his gaze. "I . . . I heard it hurts."

"The first time, for women," he said. "But not much."

She gave him a tremulous little smile, thanks for his truthfulness. The subject of pain made her glance at his scar, and he submitted himself once again to a silent examination, poised still and silent on one elbow above her.

When she reached once more to pull his head down for a kiss, there was no more need for words.

Two nights later, Victor sipped his port without tasting it, and barely managed to remain civil to his father-in-law. They had been closeted for two hours after supper, making final the details of how the money Victor had offered toward improvements of the Dorcaster farm was best to be used. It was normally a topic that would have held Victor's interest, but tonight visions of Lucianne intruded repeatedly. Lucy, in his arms. Lucy, on the bed. Lucy, reaching up to kiss him.

"I am going to bed," Reuben said around a yawn.

"So shall I," Victor said at once, putting aside his snifter and springing to his feet.

He was fairly certain he'd said good night to Reuben and his father-in-law, but he wasted little energy on worrying over the matter as he took the stairs three at a time.

Outside her door, he hesitated. This would be his third night in a row with her, he thought. Would she welcome him yet again? Did he ask too much of her? Could he possibly act any more like a randy schoolboy?

He leaned his forehead against the door and took a couple of deep breaths, which helped not at all.

The trouble was, he'd been too long celibate. He'd taken to preferring abstinence over yet again repeating how he'd gotten his scar, since to lie about it was a small but real betrayal to himself, and any woman would always ask.

No, that was nonsense. The trouble was, he was married and now that Lucy was willing—

That thought deserved to remain unfinished.

So then, the trouble was that she'd touched his scar. She'd paralyzed him with a simple caress, had put a spell over him. While that was true enough, the *real* trouble, he admitted in a tiny corner of his mind, was that he loved his wife.

He'd lain with other women. He knew what release was all about, release of the body. But he'd never held a woman he cherished, and God help him, he cherished Lucianne.

He'd been attracted to her for years, but it was more than that. That was about beauty and demeanor, but it was neither of those things that had wrapped around his heart. It was her kindness, her compassion, her ability to laugh at herself. It was the intelligence in her gaze, her unwillingness to deceive, her poise in times of difficulty.

When he held her, she filled his every sense. When he was away from her, he ached in a dozen different ways. When his body blended with hers, physical beauty meant nothing and her essence meant everything. She could be as scarred as he and he'd love her.

So why do I stand here outside her door? he asked himself, knowing he'd look a fool if anyone came along and found him with his forehead pressed to his wife's door. But what was a little foolishness compared to the question he asked himself?

He knew the answer: He was afraid. Afraid that

she could never come to love him, afraid that she welcomed him to her bed out of duty and nothing else.

Two hands slipped over his eyes from behind, and he felt breasts pressing into his back. "Guess who?" Lucy said. He spun to find her yet on tiptoe, a smile on her face. "You peeked," she teased.

God love me, if the look she's giving me is out of mere duty, then it might just be enough, Victor thought, his mouth suddenly dry with the intensity of his longing.

He reached for her, scooping her into his arms, almost making her drop the book she'd tucked under her arm. "Victor!" she squealed, then laughed.

He pushed open thc door, kicked it shut behind them, and carried her to the bed. She'd learned much the first night, but not as much as last night. He could almost laugh, remembering the look of surprise on her face when her duty had delivered pleasure, but he was too eager for what tonight could mean to be able to linger long over humor.

He was just so glad that there was to be a tonight, that she helped him untie the ties of her nightrail, that she reached for him. That was enough.

In her sleep, she cuddled against him, even though she'd refused to meet his eyes earlier. She'd closed her eyes mostly, but when they'd flown open in wonder or surprise, she'd slid her gaze to one side, not able to look him full in the face as she had only last night.

He consoled himself with the thought that there was time. With time . . .

He'd accepted the offer of her body—how could he demand yet more? But he wanted more. He needed more.

He did not ease his body away from hers. He did not want to disturb her, but it was more than that. He did not want to retreat. She was worth fighting for, worth risking his stubborn pride over. She was worth losing the sense of himself he'd shielded from everyone else.

He could leave things as they were, or he could give them time and hope, and time and his wooing, and more time. He could be patient. He could want her, and live for the day she truly wanted him.

He longed to return to Oxenby Hall. They could bake bread together if she liked, walk the fields and play chess, and raise merry, fat babies with gray-green eyes. Surely a woman would come to love the father of her children?

But children and Oxenby Hall were ages away, for Lucy had a duty to her sister first, a duty that put her in the company of the one man Victor least wanted her to see again, the one man who was everything Victor was not. Holden was handsome, blue-blooded, received by everyone, and revered as an original.

Of course, Lucy would not be the woman he thought she was if she stood in the way of an engagement between Holden and Rebecca merely because she could not bear to lose a conquest to her sister.

That was not his Lucy, no. Victor kissed the top of her head where she lay upon his shoulder, closing his eyes with mingled pleasure and pain when she stirred against him. She felt so right there beside him. How could he go on if he knew she cared yet for another man? Could he bear it if he was allowed to look into her eyes and saw they were filled with regret?

It was the fear of regrets that kept him awake long into the night.

Chapter 14

At midday the next day, Rebecca swept into the house all abustle, home from her trip to Brighton. She stepped right past Lucianne with only a passing kiss to her sister's cheek as a greeting.

"I cannot linger," Rebecca explained. "I am going driving with Mr. Ellis."

Lucy glanced out one of the front windows, seeing a carriage waited there. "But you just arrived home!" she said, trailing in her sister's wake. "I need to speak with you. Mr. Ellis can wait a moment. I'll just go and ask him to wait in the parlor—"

"That's not Mr. Ellis's coach. That is my friend's. We are going to meet Mr. Ellis." Rebecca said at once, catching Lucy's hand. She dragged her sister near and whispered in her ear. "Come with me. I have a secret. Quickly, before Mama comes to find me."

They went up to Rebecca's room, Rebecca leading the way with haste and a kind of giddiness evident in her every movement. She shut the door behind them and turned at once to Lucy. "I am eloping!" she whispered, filled with glee.

"Oh, Rebecca, no!" Lucy said at once. "Mr. Holden is not the man you think—"

"Not Mr. Holden," Rebecca said on a giggle. "Mr. Ellis!"

"Oh," Lucy said, instantly relieved. Her relief turned to chagrin however. "But, Rebecca, why an elopement? You cannot wish to begin your married life with a blemish against you. It is not done, and you know that very well. You can have a lovely church ceremony—"

"I was going to accept Mr. Holden if you approved," Rebecca interrupted. "But now I don't have to. Now I can wed where my preference lies." She blushed, proving her choice of Mr. Ellis was more than a "preference." "Your husband guaranteed my dowry, Lucianne. There is no reason I cannot accept Mr. Ellis . . . Thomas." She blushed again, clearly delighted by the sound of Mr. Ellis's Christian name on her lips.

"I married under the oddest of circumstances, Rebecca, I know, so perhaps you think that an elopement pales in comparison, but I think you ought to give this some second thought—"

"I do not want to put Papa to any expense. I want to help, not cost him more when a formal wedding is not necessary."

"Rebecca—"

"Mr. Ellis is waiting for me," Rebecca said with finality, and Lucy knew there would be no talking her sister out of her decision.

"Then I must offer my felicitations," Lucy said on a sigh, slipping her arms around her little sister for a hug. After a long minute she pushed away, gazing into Rebecca's face. "You came home to tell me so the family would not worry where you were?"

"Yes, and to pack some more gowns. I only brought three to go to Brighton. It is a long way to Gretna Green, and I want to look pretty for Thomas," Rebecca said, her cheeks flaring pink once more.

The distance was the source of the scandal, as

much as anything, of course, for it would take at least three nights on the road before Rebecca and Mr. Ellis would reach their destination in Scotland. Rebecca had decided, though, and Lucy did not doubt that Mr. Ellis would truly marry her sister. They had met the first day Rebecca debuted in society, and their mutual attraction had been obvious ever since.

It was rather unlike the man, though, to *elope* . . . Perhaps Mr. Ellis had heard that Jerome had been attempting to court Rebecca, and he wanted to make her his wife as soon as possible, before Jerome could make any headway in that regard?

Since Rebecca must carry a small portmanteau into the coach with her, an article difficult to explain to neighbors or disapproving parents, it would hardly serve for the sisters to exchange hugs at the front of the house. They clasped each other in Rebecca's room after the gowns were packed, and sniffed back tears, then finally let each other go.

"Take care. Be happy," Lucy said, waving her sister out of the room. Rebecca slipped out, still sniffling back happy tears, and Lucy pressed her hands to her face, struggling for composure. Mama would be furious when she found out, not least because she was to be denied yet another daughter's wedding ceremony.

Lucy slowly followed in Rebecca's wake, coming to the front windows just in time to see the coach turn off their street. She also saw Victor in his top hat and greatcoat, just returning on foot from some excursion he'd gone on, staring after the coach.

The butler, Coombs, opened one of the front doors for Lucy, and she stepped to Victor's side. He gave her a smile in greeting, which quickly slipped away as he gazed back in the direction the coach had disappeared. "Are you aware your sister was just here, and that she was carrying a portmanteau into that coach?" he asked over his shoulder.

"We spoke. She is eloping."

Victor spun to face her. "With Holden?"

"No. Her friend Eliza Crawford is taking her to where Mr. Ellis is waiting for her."

"Then why is she in Holden's coach?"

"That is Eliza's coach," Lucy said, but a terrible feeling snatched at her.

"It is not. It had the Broadwater crest on it."

Broadwater. The title Jerome would one day hold, if his brother did not survive. Eliza Crawford would have no reason to use a coach from the Broadwater stables . . . Rebecca had said "my friend"—and Lucy had assumed she'd meant Eliza . . .

"Holden! Could he really mean to take her to Mr. Ellis?" Lucy said on a gasp.

"Doubtful," Victor said grimly.

Lucy stared after the coach. "Could he mean to elope with Rebecca himself?"

Victor gave her a speaking glance. "If she is lucky."

"Oh, Victor," Lucy cried, understanding dawning. "Oh, he cannot mean to *ruin* her, can he?"

"That might be his intention."

"But why?"

Victor took her arm and marched them both toward the mews. "For lust. For the dowry I've provided her. For revenge against you. For spite. I don't know why, I only know we must act, and now."

"Of course," Lucy responded at once. They must quickly have a coach harnessed and pursue Holden and Rebecca. If done quickly, such folly could be overturned. A light, fast carriage like a phaeton or a curricle would be best for speed, but the discretion of a closed landau or a coach might prove important.

A coach is what Victor ordered readied as soon as they stepped into the stables. He turned to Lucy. "Get at least two cloaks, one for yourself and one for Rebecca, with hoods. They will be making for the Great North Road, I should imagine. At least until they are clear of London, Holden will want to give the impression that he is taking her to Mr. Ellis, who would in Rebecca's mind be logically waiting at a location north of the city. If Holden's intention is to seduce, I doubt he'd spare his comfort, so he must have some eventual destination in mind somewhere north."

A terrible picture flashed through Lucy's mind, an image of Rebecca being attacked in the coach, her virtue roughly and cruelly stolen. That image was quickly replaced by thoughts of the same result, only now in some nasty little inn or perhaps a hunting box or cottage . . . Rebecca would believe Jerome Holden was a man of his word, would believe he was taking her to meet with Mr. Ellis. She'd be so trusting . . .

"How will we ever find her?" she cried, shuddering in horror.

"They have not gone far," Victor tried to assure her, but she heard how grim his tone remained. He turned back to the scrambling grooms. "Prepare a horse as well," he ordered.

Lucy nodded. "That is an excellent idea. I can ride so much faster on a horse than in a coach. It gives me an advantage over them—"

"You are to get the cloaks and ride in the coach," Victor stated emphatically. His eyes had gone a bit more round than usual, and a line of perspiration appeared on his upper lip. "Head north. Have your driver ask after me—my scar will be memorable, of course."

"Victor, no!" she cried. He meant to ride after Rebecca himself! "The coach is sufficient—"

"Speed is our only advantage."

"Then let me ride after them," she pleaded.

"I can thrash Holden to within an inch of his life. You cannot," Victor said with calm logic. "I'll get Rebecca and we will wait for you at one of the inns along the way. It would seem odd for her to ride behind me, and she may be overset anyway. She'll want your calming presence and the concealment of the coach."

Just then a groom led a horse forward, saddled and readied. The lad looked to Victor, who went pale.

"Victor, do you even know how to ride?" she protested.

"No, but that is not going to stop me." He leaned forward, pressed his mouth to Lucy's for a quick kiss, and for a long moment closed his eyes, leaning down to rest his forehead on the top of her head. He opened his eyes again, gave the softest of sighs, and stepped to the horse.

His mounting lacked grace, but he ended in the saddle, the reins gripped in white-knuckled hands. He looked to Lucy, but she thought he must not be able to speak, for his throat worked and he said nothing.

He merely kicked the horse, which danced forward, its tail and head tossing, aware as horses were that its rider was too uncertain to be in charge. For one long moment Lucy thought Victor would be pitched from the animal's back, and she longed to tell him how to give the horse more subtle messages with his hands and knees. Victor put his heels to the horse again, however, and this time the animal responded by leaping into a canter.

Lucy put her hands over her mouth, as if to hold

back the protests Victor had refused to hear, and felt tears slipping down her cheeks as he rode away. She watched until he turned at the same corner the coach had taken, a wide turn that showed the horse was nearly more in charge than the rider.

"My lady?" one of the grooms inquired. "Your coach is ready."

"Yes," she responded at once. She was a fool to be merely standing there. Victor wanted her to follow, and follow she would, not just for Rebecca's sake, but in case Victor should come to harm. "I must get some cloaks," she told the groom. "I'll be right back."

She fled to the house, sending up a prayer that Victor would keep his seat, that the panic would not overwhelm him. As she gathered an armful of cloaks from the pegs in the anteroom just off the main hall, she quickly lied to a startled Coombs that she and Rebecca were going for a drive. She sent up another prayer that today's events would amount to little more than that, and shocked Coombs further by running out the front door without waiting for his assistance.

Lucy heard the familiar calls that her coachman shouted at his horses as they approached a stopping place. "Here now! Here now!" he cried out, and she could envision him planting his feet for leverage against pulling back on the ribbons, even as she felt the vehicle slowing. Her heart leaped into her throat—had Rebecca been found? Or had one of their horses gone lame? Or, heaven forbid, had the driver spotted an unseated or injured Victor?

She'd been watching out the windows, spying anxiously for the sight of a man thrown into a ditch, or a horse without a rider. She could scarce believe Victor had managed to mount the horse, let alone ride it. Did his dread build even as he rode? Would he at some point be able to bear no more, and cast himself from the saddle?

Why had he done it? Lucy wondered. It was true that she could pose no physical threat to Holden. But if Victor met up with Holden, would he be in any shape to pose a threat himself? He could have ridden with her. She ought to have suggested a faster carriage . . .

They were following the proper direction at any rate, she knew, for her coachman had had no trouble with innkeepers or farm tenants who remembered a scarred man passing by. And now they were slowing, which must be a good sign, she thought, please let it be a good sign.

She spied Victor's horse, knowing it by the white stocking on its rear left leg, tied before a small inn with a sign declaring it THE THRUSH. Victor was nowhere in sight.

As soon as the coach stopped, Lucy threw open the door and climbed down unassisted. She flew to the inn's door, vastly disappointed to find no one but the innkeeper in the common room.

"More of the Quality?" the innkeeper asked, already pointing to a rickety set of stairs.

Lucy nodded to him and ran to the stairs, calling back over her shoulder, "Which door?"

"Second to the right," the man called up to her.

The door stood open. Silence met her straining ears, causing her to slow her steps and approach the doorway with caution.

She glanced around the doorjamb and saw a man sprawled on the floor. Her first impulse was to dash into the room, afraid it was Victor, overcome, but she stopped abruptly. It was Jerome Holden, and his lower lip was split, spilling drops of scarlet onto his cravat.

Over him stood Mr. Ellis, and next to Mr. Ellis, Victor. Behind Victor, Rebecca peeked out, a look of ferocious satisfaction on her face.

"You'll want to mind that lip, Holden," Victor advised, his voice droll. "It might leave a scar."

"Rebecca . . . ?" Lucy said, stepping into the room and grabbing the attention of everyone. "Victor?"

Rebecca looked up, gave a low moan, and rushed into Lucy's arms. "It was Mr. Ellis. He hit him. And he was awful. And he was going to make Mr. Ellis believe that I was a . . . a *fallen* woman! And I hope he goes to Hades!" Rebecca said rather incoherently just before dissolving into tears.

"Mr. Ellis?" Lucy echoed, unsure which "he" and "him" Rebecca meant. She patted Rebecca on the back and let her sob on her shoulder, and looked to Victor for answers.

"I believe your sister wishes Mr. Holden to Hades, not Mr. Ellis who has, as you can see, just drawn the man's claret," Victor said.

"Whatever is Mr. Ellis doing here?" Lucy asked, moving to help Rebecca sit in a chair. Apparently any fisticuffs had not involved Victor, whom Lucy was hugely relieved to see was whole and well and none the worse for having ridden a horse.

"Holden told him to come here," Victor said. "Holden told both Lady Rebecca and Mr. Ellis that each of the other wished to elope, and arranged it so that Mr. Ellis would wait here for Rebecca to be delivered by Holden. I arrived after Mr. Ellis, but fortunately in good time, for I was able to assure him that Lady Rebecca was innocent in all this."

Victor crossed to Lucy's side with a handkerchief ready to hand to her, which she handed to Rebecca.

"But why did Mr. Holden want Mr. Ellis here at all?" Lucy asked in confusion.

"Holden knew Lady Rebecca was in love with Mr. Ellis. With her dowry restored, she was free to marry as her heart dictated," Victor explained. "But if Mr. Ellis should happen to come to this inn and should happen to find Lady Rebecca in the arms of another man . . ."

"But *why?*" Lucy repeated, this time to Holden. He had come to his knees, gingerly dabbing his lip with his fingers, but now he stood, dusting himself off with the hauteur of an offended cat.

When the man did not answer her, Lucy went on. "Mr. Holden, I cannot believe that you are so anxious for income that there is no other woman in the world who would suit for marriage but my sister," she said coldly.

"Indeed, I have no need for whatever paltry sum comes with your sister's hand," Holden answered just as coldly. He ran his tongue over his lower lip and grimaced.

"Then why?" Lucy demanded. "Revenge? Against me?"

"You flatter yourself," he said with a sneer, and she believed him. Simple revenge was not motivation enough for him. Jealousy or anger that she'd rejected him and Victor had been the one to marry her was perhaps some small part of it. Assuaging his pride might have been yet more reason, but it was not the primary impetus.

She understood his reasoning, for Jerome Holden was nothing if he was not consistent in his unpredictability.

"You did it because you thought you could. Because it amused you. Because it was unexpected," she said, horror creeping up her spine at the cold-bloodedness of it.

"I wouldn't have ruined her. I would have married her," Holden pointed out. "Probably."

"Saint Jerome." It was Victor's turn to sneer.

"I would have so enjoyed family gatherings," Holden said with a reptilian smile as he loosed his cravat. He frowned down at the bloodied cloth. "This is entirely ruined," he said, tossing it to the floor with disgust.

Another fist slammed into the man's face, sending him unconscious to the floor. Victor looked up, fist still clenched, knuckles turned red from the impact.

"I didn't care to hear what else he had to say," he explained, looking askance at Lucy. If he was concerned that she would disapprove, she was sure the feral gratification she allowed into her gaze disabused him of the idea. His features relaxed, and he sent back a smile that was just as feral as he rubbed his knuckles.

"What now?" Mr. Ellis asked into the sudden silence. "It seems to me that all this will be dashed difficult to smooth over. I told friends that my lady love wanted to elope tonight. I was happy. I . . . I believed Mr. Holden's lies."

Lucy looked at him with a kind of hopeless amusement, for in love he'd proven as gullible as Rebecca, and his gullibility had made it that much harder to protect her sister's good name.

Mr. Ellis looked to Lucy, and Rebecca to Victor, and everyone got the same pinched look upon their faces as they tried to think of a solution.

"If not an elopement," Victor said after several long moments, "what about a marriage?"

"What?" Rebecca and Lucy said together.

"Mr. Ellis, would you be willing to wed Lady Rebecca tonight?"

Mr. Ellis stared, but then he slowly nodded. "Yes,"

he said quietly, then repeated the word, louder, "Yes."

"Would you marry Mr. Ellis, Lady Rebecca?"

Her eyes were wide under the fringe of dark hair across her forehead. "Yes. Of course, yes."

Victor turned to Lucy. "I believe your godmama owes us a favor, my dear."

It was bordering on half an hour since Rebecca had taken on a new name, Lady Rebecca Ellis, when the coach containing her, her brand-new husband, her sister, and her brother-in-law pulled up before Dorcaster House. Lady Rebecca and her new husband preceded Victor and Lucy from the carriage, intent on waiting in the parlor in order to tell Lord and Lady Dorcaster their news. Victor and Lucy sat still within the coach each blowing out a breath in relief that this day was coming to a conclusion.

"I don't believe I will ever be able to present myself again at Lambeth Palace," Victor said as he belatedly stepped out of the coach and turned to hand Lucy down. "At least not when the archbishop is in residence."

"Even should you have a third special request written in the queen's hand?" Lucy suggested.

"Especially under those circumstances."

Lucy laughed as they approached the front of the house.

"It is getting crowded in this house," he pointed out, opening the door for his wife.

"And in the rear parlor, unless I mishear the direction of voices." There was indeed a babble of voices coming from the recesses of the house.

"Should we join them?" Victor asked.

"For supper," Lucy suggested, "but not now."

Victor removed his hat and greatcoat, handing

them to Coombs, who belatedly arrived in the front hall. The butler was too dignified to comment on the news being delivered in the parlor, but a hint of a smile revealed that he'd overheard the news. "Shall I show you to the rear parlor, my lord, my lady?" Coombs asked.

"No," Lucy answered for them both. "But will you please send a ewer of hot water to our chambers?"

"Very good, ma'am," Coombs said, bowing.

Lucy reached for Victor's hand and pulled him toward the stairs. "You must put up your leg with a hot compress, so it won't ache."

"Then you'll have to put compresses on my entire body. I never knew how painful it is to ride a horse! I'm certain my bruises have bruises."

Lucy clucked her tongue, still amazed he had done it. "I was thinking more of putting compresses on your brow."

"My brow?" Victor asked as she led him toward her chamber door.

She glanced back at him, feeling shy, not knowing how to ask the question in her mind. Honesty might be best. It was difficult to not be honest with Victor . . . to not look into his eyes when he made love to her, not let him see what was in her heart.

"I thought that after the . . . the ride you took today, that you might feel upset. Is it too late for soothing compresses to the brow? Would they help?"

He did not answer her. When they were in their room and the door closed behind him, he stepped away from her to fiddle with the fire. She smothered a sigh; she'd hoped he would take her into his arms, not take offense. Had his sacrifice today, his bravery, come at a terrible cost?

"It was appalling," he finally said, quietly, with his back to her as he knelt on one knee before the fire. "I thought I was going to die, that my heart would just give out. I hated every moment I was on that animal's back."

"But you did it, you rode. You found Rebecca. You kept Mr. Ellis from believing the wrong thing."

He stood slowly with a little grunt of pain and frowned thoughtfully down at the fire. He gave a small, rueful laugh. "Despite it all, though, I am still not the man that Holden is."

Lucy stepped to his side, putting her hand on his arm to force Victor to turn to her, sure her gaze had to be sparking with anger. "You're twice the man Holden is."

"The fear—"

"Is nothing compared to the awfulness that is in Holden! He is a corrupted, evil man. So he can ride twenty horses a day and never show an ounce of fear! I would that he had some fear in him, something to make him human, to make him care how he treats people."

"You sound as if you do not care for the man," Victor tried to quip, but he succeeded only in gaining a punch in the arm for his trouble. "Ow!" he said, almost laughing, covering the spot with his other hand.

"That is for thinking I could care one jot for Jerome Holden," Lucy said warmly.

"Lucy," Victor said, still half laughing, moving his hands to her upper arms and leaning into her so that his chin could rest on her head. "You are right. I know better. You could never care for a man of so little depth."

"Never."

He was very quiet and still for several long heartbeats, which she felt beneath her cheek where she leaned into his chest. "And where does that leave me?" he whispered.

"In my bed?" she suggested.

She felt his low laugh, and felt him kiss the top of her head, but it was an oddly sad gesture. She abruptly went up on tiptoe, slipping her arms around his neck, forcing his gaze to meet her own, afraid in some primal way that he was slipping away from her.

She kept her eyes open, let her heart into them, let him see what she could not quite find the words to say. He must know, for she could not pretend any longer. It would be better to live apart as soon as possible if he could not bear her love for him. She'd meant to be a good wife to him, to hide her love, to gladden his days if she could not gladden his heart—but she could not do it. She could not lic in his arms and hide her feelings behind closed eyes, not for the rest of her life, not for another day.

"Lucy." He repeated her name, but there was something of awe now in his voice, something of hope.

Lucy laughed, but it sounded more like a sob—he was glad, oh, she could tell that he was gladdened by what she had let him see.

"Say it," he said, his voice low and a little shaky. "I want to believe my ruined face means nothing to you, that my mania is—"

She put her mouth to his, to stop his words, but not to kiss him. "I love you," she whispered against his lips. From there she could not see into his gaze, from there he could not misunderstand her meaning. She'd dared to say the words, and now he would take what she offered or crush her heart entirely.

His arms slid around her, pulling the rest of her as close as her lips, their breath mingling, as intimate as their bodies had been just the night before.

"I love you, too," he whispered against her mouth.

They pulled apart, to look at each other, and

then they were laughing and kissing at the same time, a joyous, frenzied exchange of wonder and delight.

The ringing of the supper bell caused them to pause between kisses.

"We should dress for supper," Victor said, his voice hoarse.

"Are you hungry?" Lucy asked, and blushed at the look that came into his eyes.

"Very."

"Me, too," she said, reaching to pull one of the tapes of her gown undone.

He grinned wolfishly at her. "Very, very hungry," he said as he scooped her into his arms and carried her to the bed.

It was easy to play at lovemaking, but when Victor's body came into hers, Lucy rejoiced that she could open her eyes and meet his squarely, could let him see the love that made their marriage real.

Queen Charlotte's coach pulled before her home, just returned from the church where Rebecca Gordon had abruptly married one Mr. Thomas Ellis. She and her attending lady-in-waiting, Marjorie Fewersham, waited for the door of the coach to be opened and the steps let down.

"That was a very . . . sudden wedding," Marjorie said from her seat. "It is a good thing Dorcaster has no more daughters, or they might feel compelled to find ever more exotic ways in which to marry."

"True," conceded the queen.

The door opened, and the steps were let down, and the ladies were handed from the carriage by a footman in royal livery. The queen led, and Marjorie followed, dressed in the blue gown required of all the queen's ladies-in-waiting, with its red collar and brass buttons.

As they walked toward the queen's private apartments, Charlotte shooed away a bevy of attendants, summoning only Marjorie forth with her.

"I daresay Mr. Holden was most distressed to be banned from all future royal assemblies and parties," Marjorie said conversationally as they walked past grand paintings in gilded frames. "His papa will be most upset."

"We reap what we sow," the queen stated.

"However do you suppose Holden received that split lip?"

"He earned it, I daresay."

"You do not mean to tell me why, do you?" Marjorie asked.

"I do not."

Marjorie shrugged. There were many things the queen did not explain to Marjorie, nor any of her ladies. Marjorie did know one of the queen's secrets, though.

"I daresay Lord and Lady Oxenby look well together, do they not?" she said now, sliding the queen a smug look.

Marjorie was the only one of the queen's ladies who knew that Lady Lucianne Gordon's name had been a prearranged detail of the masquerade. The queen had only seen fit to tell her because Marjorie had accidentally seen another name on the slip of paper the queen had drawn.

"Why do you not require spectacles?" Queen Charlotte had grumbled at her before she'd taken Marjorie aside, sworn her to secrecy, and revealed her little secret.

"I think Lord Oxenby might well be the perfect complement for Lucianne Gordon, do you not, ma'am? It is a very fortunate thing that you pulled his name from the bowl that night at the masquerade," Marjorie said.

"Do try not to be a ninny, Marjorie," Queen Charlotte said primly as they entered her dressing room and she handed her fan and bonnet to Marjorie.

"Ma'am?"

The queen sat down at her dressing table, lifting a foot so that her slipper might be removed. She must dress for supper at eight—perhaps she'd even choose to sup tonight.

"Of course they suit. Of course I drew Oxenby's name. Drawing his name was as prearranged as hers had been."

She waggled her foot at Marjorie and just managed to hide a smug smile of her own at the look of complete surprise on the lady's face.

Signet Regency Romances

BROKEN PROMISES
by Patricia Oliver

A widow returns to London and gets reacquainted with the man she left at the altar ten years earlier. Could this be a second chance for love—or a scheme for revenge?

0-451-20296-1/$4.99

THE UNSUITABLE MISS MARTINGALE
by Barbara Hazard

Sent to London by her family in hopes that she will marry respectably, Lili Martingalc finds herself out of place in London high society. But she has a place in the heart of Viscount Halpern...

0-451-20265-1/$4.99

LORD DRAGONER'S WIFE
by Lynn Kerstan

When the scandalous Lord Dragoner returns to England, Delilah's hopes of a reconciliation are shattered. The husband who coldly abandoned her has come to seek a divorce. But she is determined to win his heart, even if it means joining him in the dangerous world where no one can be trusted—not even his wife.

0-451-19861-1/$4.99

To order call: 1-800-788-6262

The Beleaguered Earl by Allison Lane

Hope Ashburton was dismayed to learn that her family home had been gambled away to a disreputable earl. But the new owner, the notorious Maxwell Longford, seemed genuinely interested in restoring her ruined estate—and stealing her heart, as well....

0-451-19972-3/$4.99

The Rebellious Twin by Shirley Kennedy

Clarinda and Clarissa Capelle are identical twins—but when it comes to social graces, they're complete opposites. Especially when they both fall in love...with the same handsome Lord!

0-451-19899-9/$4.99

To order call: 1-800-788-6262